THINKING DOUBLE

With eyes closed he carefully reviewed the situation. He was in a cell with rock walls at least four feet thick. The only openings were a narrow gap blocked by five massive steel bars and an armor-plated door in constant view of patrolling guards.

Thirty, forty, or fifty Rigellians working in a patient, determined group might tunnel under the wall and both illuminated areas and get away. But he had one resource and one only. That was guile.

He let go a loud groan and complained to himself, "So I'll have to use both my heads!"

After a while he sat up startled, and said in a tone approaching a yelp, "Yes, sure, that's it—*both* heads!"

By Eric Frank Russell
Published by Ballantine Books:

THE BEST OF ERIC FRANK RUSSELL

NEXT OF KIN

SENTINELS FROM SPACE

SINISTER BARRIER

THREE TO CONQUER

WASP

NEXT OF KIN

Eric Frank Russell

A Del Rey Book

BALLANTINE BOOKS • NEW YORK

A Del Rey Book
Published by Ballantine Books

ISBN 0-345-32761-6

Printed in Canada

First Ballantine Books Edition: April 1986
Second Printing: September 1987

Cover Art by Barclay Shaw

Introduction

by Jack L. Chalker*

It is ironic that Eric Frank Russell (1905–1978) is best known in the United States for two novels that were never published in this country in the form in which he wrote them—until now that is.

Russell wrote *Next of Kin* in 1955 intending it as a serial for *Astounding Science Fiction*, since most of his work during his long SF writing career appeared there, with hopes of a later publication in book form. At this time, however, John Campbell, editor of *Astounding*, was over-inventoried on novels for serialization; most SF magazines had collapsed between 1953 and 1955, so the few survivors, like *Astounding*, were inundated with material. Campbell liked the story very much; he always liked Russell's work. He simply had

*Jack L. Chalker is a popular science fiction and fantasy author who has been a long-time admirer of the works of Eric Frank Russell and who feels that Russell was a strong influence on his own writing. Most of the facts used in this introduction came from letters written by Russell over the years to Chalker and mutual friends. Chalker's enthusiasm was instrumental in bringing about Del Rey's revival of Russell's work.

no room for it in *Astounding*'s publishing schedule. But being one of the great editors of fiction of this century, he saw within the novel a strong section that could stand on its own, and he suggested that Russell rewrite these parts and transform them into a novelette he would buy. Feeling that he could get the completed book published later, Russell agreed and complied, with Campbell titling the tale "Plus X." It was highly acclaimed and was one of *Astounding*'s most popular stories.

When Russell's U.S. agent tried to market the completed *Next of Kin*, however, he struck a deal with Ace Books which at that time was publishing the famous Ace doubles — two short novels, each around 40,000 words, in one volume. Don Wollheim, then Ace's editor, wanted the book, but he had to stick to the format. He suggested that Russell write a longer version of "Plus X," to about 40,000 words. If Russell did so, Ace would then include a collection of Russell short stories on the flip side. Russell did so, and as a result we had the Wollheim-titled *The Space Willies* on one side, and a good collection, *Six Worlds Yonder*, on the other. Still, however, *Next of Kin* in its complete and original form found no home in the U.S. (although it was published in the United Kingdom, where it continues as a perennial seller).

The book you are holding is the first U.S. publication of the novel as Russell wrote it and as, up to now, it was read in the U.S. only by editors. It is in the family of stories that also includes *Wasp* and shorter works like *Diabologic*, *The Waitabits*, and other space exploration and war stories of Russell's. It is a wonderful, fun, fast yarn that hasn't aged a bit, and it never, never takes itself seriously. Indeed, Russell, who was a Fortean and whose first novel, *Sinister Barrier*, dealt very seriously with that subject, even manages to poke fun at the "we are property" concept — and all the other themes he held dear over the years.

Chapter 1

He knew he'd stuck his neck out and it was too late to withdraw. It had been the same since early childhood when he'd accepted dares and been sorry immediately afterward. They say that one learns from experience; if that were true the human race would now be devoid of folly. He'd learned plenty in his time and forgotten most of it within a week. So yet again he'd wangled himself into a predicament and undoubtedly would be left to wangle himself out of it as best he could.

Once more he knocked at the door, a little harder but not imperatively. Behind the panels a chair scraped and a harsh voice responded with hearable impatience.

"Come in!"

Marching inside, he stood at attention before the desk, head erect, thumbs in line with the seams of the pants, feet at an angle of forty-five degrees. A robot, he thought, just a damned robot.

1

Fleet-Admiral Markham surveyed him from beneath bushy brows, his cold gaze slowly rising from feet to head then descending from head to feet.

"Who are you?"

"Scout-Officer John Leeming, sir."

"Oh, yes." Markham maintained the stare then suddenly barked, "Button your fly."

Leeming jerked and showed embarrassment. "I can't, sir. It has a defective zipper."

"Then why haven't you visited the tailor? That's what the base tailor-shop is for, isn't it? Does your commanding officer approve of his men appearing before me sloppily dressed? I doubt it! What the devil do you mean by it?"

"I haven't had time to tend to it, sir. The zipper packed up only a few minutes ago," explained Leeming.

"Is that so?" Fleet-Admiral Markham lay back in his chair and scowled at nothing. "There's a war on, a galactic war. To fight it successfully and to win it we are wholly dependent upon our space-navies. It's a hell of a thing when the navy goes into battle with defective zippers."

Since he seemed to expect a reply to that one, Leeming gave it. "With all respect, sir, I don't see that it matters. During a battle a man doesn't care what happens to his pants so long as he survives intact."

"I agree," said Markham. "But what worries me is the question of how much other and more important material may prove to be substandard. If civilian contractors fail on little things they'll certainly fail on big ones. Such failures can cost lives."

"Yes, sir," said Leeming, wondering what the other was getting at.

"A new and untried ship, for instance," Markham went on. "If it operates as planned, well and good. If it doesn't——" He let the sentence peter out, thought awhile, continued, "We asked for volunteers for special long-range reconnaissance patrols. You were the first to hand in your name. I want to know why."

"If the job has to be done somebody must do it," answered Leeming evasively.

"I am fully aware of the fact. But I want to know exactly why you volunteered." He waited a bit, urged, "Come on, speak up! I won't penalise a risk-taker for giving his reasons."

Thus encouraged, Leeming said, "I like action. I like working on my own. I don't like the time-wasting discipline they go in for around the base. It gives me a pain in the seat. Stand here, stand there, put your chest out, pull your belly in, polish your shoes, get a haircut, take that silly look off your face, who'd you think you're speaking to? I'm a fully trained scout pilot and not a dressed-up dummy for uniformed loudmouths to bark at. I want to get on with the work for which I am suited and that's all there is to it."

Markham showed no ire. On the contrary, he nodded understandingly. "So do most of us. Terrans always were an impatient bunch. Do you think I'm not frustrated sitting behind a desk while a major war is being fought?" Without waiting for a response he added, "I've no time for a man who volunteers because he's been crossed in love or wants to do some heavy bragging or anything like that. I want a competent pilot who is an individualist afflicted with the fidgets."

"Yes, sir."

"You seem to fit the part all right. Your technical record is first-class. Your disciplinary record stinks to high heaven." He eyed his listener blank-faced. "Two charges of refusing to obey a lawful order. Four for insolence and insubordination. One for parading with your cap on back to front. What on earth made you do that?"

"I had a bad attack of what-the-hell, sir," explained Leeming.

"Did you? Well, it's obvious that you're a confounded nuisance. The space-base would be better off without you."

"Yes, sir."

"As you know, we and a few allies are fighting a big combine led by the Lathians. The size of the opposition doesn't worry us. What we lack in numbers we more than make up for in competence and efficiency. Our war-potential is great and rapidly growing greater. We'll skin the Lathians alive before we're through."

Leeming offered no comment, having become tired of yessing.

"We've one serious weakness," Markham informed. "We lack adequate information about the enemy's cosmic hinterland. We know how wide the Combine spreads but not how deep into the starfield it goes. It's true that the enemy is no wiser with regard to us, but that's his worry."

Again Leeming made no remark.

"Ordinary warships haven't flight-duration sufficiently prolonged to dig deep behind the Combine's spatial front. That difficulty will be overcome when we capture one or more of their outpost worlds with repair and refuelling facilities. However, we can't afford to wait until then. Our Intelligence Service wants some essential data just as soon as it can be got. Do you understand?"

"Yes, sir."

"Good! We have developed a new kind of superfast scoutship. I can't tell you how it functions except that it does not use the normal caesium-ion form of propulsion. Its type of power-unit is a top secret. For that reason it must not fall into the enemy's hands. At the last resort the pilot must destroy it even if it means also destroying himself."

"Completely wrecking a ship, though a small one, is much more difficult than it seems."

"Not this ship," Markham retorted. "She carries an effective charge in her engine-room. The pilot need but press a button to scatter the power-units piecemeal over a wide area."

"I see."

"That charge is the sole explosive aboard. The ship has not a gun, not a guided missile, no armament of any sort. It's a stripped-down vessel with everything sacrificed for the sake of speed and its only defence is to scoot good and fast. That, I assure you, it can do. Nothing in the galaxy can catch it providing it is squirting from all twenty propulsors."

"Sounds good to me, sir," approved Leeming, licking his lips.

"It is good. It's got to be good. The unanswered question is that of whether it is good enough to take the beating of a long, long trip. The tubes are the weakest part of any spaceship. Sooner or later they burn out. That's what bothers me. The tubes on this ship have very special linings. In theory they should last for months. In practice they might not. You know what that means?"

"No repairs and no replacements in enemy territory, no means of getting back," Leeming offered.

"Correct. And the vessel would have to be destroyed. From that moment the pilot, if still surviving, has isolated himself somewhere within the mists of Creation. His chance of seeing humankind again is remote enough to verge on the impossible."

"There could be worse situations. I'd rather be alive

someplace else than stone-dead here. While there's life there's hope."

"You still wish to go through with this?"

"Sure thing, sir."

"Then upon your own head be it," said Markham with grim humour. "Go along the corridor, seventh door on the right, and report to Colonel Farmer. Tell him I sent you."

"Yes, sir."

"And before you go try that damned zipper again."

Obediently, Leeming tried it. The thing slid all the way as smoothly as if oiled. He stared at the other with a mixture of astonishment and injured innocence.

"I started in the ranks and I haven't forgotten it," said Markham, pointedly. "You can't fool me."

Colonel Farmer, of Military Intelligence, was a beefy, florid-faced character who looked slightly dumb but had a sharp mind. He was examining a huge star-map hung upon one wall when Leeming walked in. Farmer swung around as if expecting to be stabbed in the back.

"Haven't you been taught to knock before you enter?"

"Yes, sir."

"Then why didn't you?"

"I forgot, sir. My mind was occupied with the interview I've just had with Fleet-Admiral Markham."

"Did he send you to me?"

"Yes, sir."

"Oh, so you're the long-range reconnaissance pilot, eh? I don't suppose Commodore Keen will be sorry to see you go. You've been somewhat of a thorn in his side, haven't you?"

"No, sir," denied Leeming. "I have been a pain in his seat—every time he's tried to sit on me."

"In the armed forces one must get used to that sort of thing."

"Sorry, sir, but I don't agree. One joins the forces to help win a war and for no other purpose. I am not a juvenile delinquent called up for reformation by the Commodore or by anyone else."

"He'd differ from you there. He's a stickler for discipline." Farmer let go a chuckle at some secret joke, added, "Keen by name and keen by nature." He contemplated the other a short while, went on more soberly, "You've picked yourself a tough job."

"That doesn't worry me," Leeming assured. "Birth, marriage and death are tough jobs."

"You might never come back."

"Makes little difference. Eventually we'll all take a ride from which we'll never come back."

"Well, you needn't mention it with such ghoulish satisfaction," Farmer complained. "Are you married?"

"No, sir. Whenever I get the urge I just lie down quietly until the feeling passes off."

Farmer eyed the ceiling and said, "God!"

"What else do you expect?" asked Leeming, displaying slight aggressiveness. "A scout-pilot operates single-handed. He's like a bug in a metal can and has to learn to dispense with a lot of things, especially companionship. It's surprising how much one can do without if one really tries."

"I'm sure," soothed Farmer. He gestured toward the star-map. "On that, the nearest points of light are arrayed across the enemy's front. The mist of stars behind them are unknown territory. The Combine may be far weaker than we think because its front is wafer-thin. Or it may be more powerful because its authority stretches far to the rear. The only way

7

to find out exactly what we're up against is to effect a deep penetration through the enemy's spatial lines."

Leeming said nothing.

"We propose to send a special scout-ship through this area where occupied worlds lie far apart, the Combine's defences are somewhat scattered and their detector devices are relatively sparse." Farmer put his finger on a dark patch on the map. "With the speed your vessel possesses, the enemy will have hardly enough time to identify you as hostile before they lose trace of you. We have every reason to believe that you'll be able to slip through into their rear without trouble."

"I hope so," contributed Leeming, seeing that a response was expected.

"The only danger point is here." Shifting his finger an inch, Farmer placed it on a bright star. "A Lathian-held solar system containing at least four large space-navy stations. If those fleets happen to be zooming around the bolt-hole they might intercept you more by accident than good judgment. So you'll be accompanied that far by a strong escort."

"That's nice."

"If the escort should become involved in a fight you will not attempt to take part. It would be futile to do so, anyway, because your vessel carries no offensive armament. You will take full advantage of the diversion to race out of range and dive through the Combine's front. Is that understood?"

"Yes, sir."

"After you get through you must use your initiative. Bear in mind that we don't want to know how far beyond there are worlds holding intelligent life—you would never reach the end of those even if you continued to the crack of doom. We want to know only how far back there are such worlds in regular communication with various members of the Combine. Whenever you come across an organised planet playing ball with the Combine you will at once transmit all the details you can offer."

"I will."

"Immediately you are satisfied that you have gained the measure of the enemy's depth you will return as quickly as possible. You must get the ship back here if it can be done. If for any reason you cannot return, the ship must be converted into scrap. No abandoning it in free space, no dumping it into an ocean or anything like that. The ship *must* be destroyed. Markham has emphasised this, hasn't he?"

"Yes, sir,"

"All right. We're giving you forty-eight hours in which to clear up your personal affairs. After that, you will report to Number Ten Spaceport." Farmer held out his hand. "I wish you all the luck you can get."

"Thinking I'll need it?" Leeming grinned and went on, "You're laying very heavy odds against ever seeing me again. It's written across your face. I'll be back—want to bet on it?"

"No," said Farmer. "I never gamble because I'm a bad loser. But if and when you do return I'll tuck you into bed with my own two hands."

"That's a promise," warned Leeming.

He went to his tiny room, found another fellow already in occupation. This character eyed him with faint embarrassment.

"You Leeming?"

"That's right."

"I'm Davies, Jack Davies."

"Glad to know you." Grabbing his bags, Leeming started

packing them, stuffing away with careless haste shirts, collars and handkerchiefs.

Sitting on the bed, Davies informed, "They told me to take over your room. They said you'd be leaving today."

"Correct."

"Going far?"

"Don't know for certain. It might be too far."

"Are you pleased to go?"

"Sure am," Leeming enthused.

"Can't say I blame you." Davies ruminated a moment in glum silence, went on, "I arrived a couple of hours ago and reported to the Base C.O. An autocratic type if ever I saw one." He gave a brief, unflattering description of Commodore Keen. "I don't know his name."

"Mallarqui," Leeming informed.

"That so? Uncommon, isn't it?"

"No." Closing the case, Leeming kneeled on its lid while he locked it, started on the next one. "It's as old as the hills. You've heard of a lot of Mallarqui, haven't you?"

"Yes, I have."

"Well, in this dump there's too much of it."

"I think you're right. Mallarqui took one look at me and yelled, 'Haircut!'" Ruefully, Davies rubbed the short bristle covering his pate. "So I went and got one. What a Space Navy! Immediately you show your face they scalp you. And what d'you suppose happened next?"

"They issued you with a brush and comb."

"They did just that." He massaged the bristle again. "What for?"

"Same reason as they do everything else," explained Leeming. "B.B.B."

"B.B.B.? What d'you mean?"

"It's a motto adopted by the boys on inactive service.

You'll find yourself reciting it about twenty times per day. Baloney Baffles Brains."

"I see," said Davies, taking on a worried look.

"The only way to escape is to fall foul of Keen. He'll get rid of you—after he's broken your heart."

"Keen? Who's he?"

"Mallarqui," corrected Leeming, hurriedly. "The fellows call him Keen behind his back. If you want to stay out of the pokey don't *ever* call him Commodore Keen to his face. He likes to be addressed as Mr. Mallarqui."

"Thanks for the tip," said Davies, innocently grateful.

"You're quite welcome. Take your butt off the bed—I want my pyjamas."

"Sorry." Davies stood up, sat down again.

Cramming the pyjamas into the case, Leeming closed it, took a long look around.

"That's about all, I guess. Victory has been postponed by sheer lack of efficient zippers. I got that information straight from the top. So they're rushing me out to win the war. From now on all you need do is sit around and count the days." He made for the door, a bag in each hand.

Coming to his feet again, Davies said awkwardly, "Happy landings."

"Thanks."

In the corridor the first person Leeming encountered was Commodore Keen. Being too burdened to salute, he threw the other a regulation eyes-left which Keen acknowledged with a curt nod. Keen brushed past and entered the room. His loud, harsh voice boosted out the open door.

"Ah, Davies, so you have settled in. Since you won't be required today you can clean up this hog-pen in readiness for my inspection this evening."

"Yes, Mr. Mallarqui."

"WHAT?"

Outside, Leeming took a firmer grip on his bags and ran like hell.

The ship was a beauty, the same diameter as an ordinary scout-vessel but over twice the length. These proportions made it look less like a one-man snoop-boat than a miniature cruiser. Standing on its tail, it towered so high that its nose seemed to reach halfway towards the clouds.

Studying it appreciatively, Leeming asked, "Any more like this?"

"Three," responded Montecelli, the spaceport's chief engineer. "All hidden elsewhere with a tight security ring around them. Strict orders from above say that this type of vessel may be used only one at a time. A second must not be sent out until after yours has returned."

"So I'm first on the list, eh? What if I don't come back? What if this ship is destroyed and you've no way of knowing?"

The other shrugged. "That's the War Staff's worry, not mine. I only obey directives from above and those can be trouble enough."

"H'm! Probably they've set a time limit for my safe return. If I'm not back by then they'll assume that I'm a gone goose."

"They haven't said anything to you about it?"

"No."

"Then don't you worry either. Life's too short. In time of war it gets shortened for many." Montecelli scowled at the sky. "Whenever a boat boosts upward on a column of flame I never know whether that'll be the last I'll ever see of it."

"That's right, cheer me on my way," said Leeming. "The life and soul of the party."

"Sorry, I clean forgot you're going." He pointed to an adjacent building. "In there we've set up a duplicate nose-cabin for training purposes. It will take you most of a week to become accustomed to the new-type controls, to learn to handle the transspatial radio and generally get the feel of things. You can start your education as soon as you like."

"All I'm bothered about is the autopilot," Leeming told him. "It had better be a good one. A fellow can't travel for days and weeks without sleep and he can't snooze with the ship running wild. A really reliable autopilot is his fairy godmother."

"Listen, son, if this one could do more than hold you on course while jerking you away from dangers, if it could see and think and transmit reports, we'd send it away without you." Montecelli gave his listener a reassuring slap on the shoulder. "It's the best ever. It'd take care of you even if you were on your honeymoon and temporarily unconscious of the cosmos."

"The only resemblance is that I'll need my strength," said Leeming. He entered the building and more or less stayed in it for the prescribed week.

The take-off came at one hour after sunset. There was a cloudless sky, velvet black and spangled with stars. Strange to think that far, far out there, concealed by sheer distance, were countless populated worlds with Combine warships parading warily between some of them while the allied fleets of Terrans, Sirians, Rigellians and others were on the prowl across an enormous front.

Below, long chains of arc-lights dithered as a gentle breeze swept across the spaceport. Beyond the safety barriers that defined the coming blast-area a group of people were waiting to witness the ascent. If the ship toppled instead of going up, thought Leeming wryly, the whole lot of them would race for sanctuary with burning backsides. It did not occur to him that in such an event he would be in poor position to enjoy the sight.

A voice came out of the tiny loudspeaker set in the cabin wall. "Warm up, Pilot."

He pressed a button. Something went *whump*, then the ship groaned and shuddered while a great circular cloud of dust and vapour rolled across the concrete and concealed the safety barriers. The low groaning and trembling continued while he sat in silence, his full attention upon the instrument bank. The needles of twenty meters crawled to the right, quivered awhile, became still. That meant steady and equal pressure in the twenty stern tubes.

"Everything all right, Pilot?"

"Yes."

"Take off at will." A pause, followed by, "Lots of luck!"

"Thanks!"

He let the tubes blow for another half minute before gradually he moved the tiny boost-lever toward him. Shuddering increased, the groan raised its pitch until it became a howl, the cabin windows misted over and the sky was obscured.

For a nerve-racking second the vessel rocked on its tail-fins. Then it began to creep upward, a foot, a yard, ten yards. The howl was now a shriek. The chronically slow rate of climb suddenly changed as something seemed to give the vessel a hearty shove in the rear. Up it went, a hundred feet, a thousand, ten thousand. Through the clouds and into the deep of the night. The cabin windows were clear, the sky was full of stars and the Moon looked huge.

The loudspeaker said in faint, squeaky tones, "Nice work, Pilot."

14

"All my work is nice," retorted Leeming. "See you in the asylum."

There was no answer to that. They knew that he'd become afflicted with an exaggerated sense of freedom referred to as take-off intoxication. Most pilots suffered from it as soon as a planet lay behind their tail and only the stars could be seen ahead. The symptoms consisted of sardonic comments and abuse raining down from the sky.

"Go get a haircut," bawled Leeming into his microphone. He jiggled around in his seat while the ship boomed onward. "And clean up that hog-pen. Haven't you been taught how to salute? Baloney baffles brains!"

They didn't answer that, either.

But down in the spaceport control-tower the duty officer pulled a face and said to Montecelli, "You know, I think that Einstein never worked out the whole of it."

"What d'you mean?"

"I have a theory that as one approaches the velocity of light one's inhibitions shrink to zero."

"You may have something there," Montecelli conceded.

"Pork and beans, pork and beans, Holy God, pork and beans," squawked the control-tower speaker with swiftly fading strength. "Get undressed because I want to test your eyes. Now inhale. Keen by name and keen by——"

The duty officer switched it off.

Chapter 2

He picked up the escort in the Sirian sector, the first encounter being made when he was fast asleep. Activated by a challenging signal on a pre-set frequency, the alarm sounded just above his ear and caused him to dive out of the bunk while no more than half awake. For a moment he gazed stupidly around while the ship vibrated and the autopilot went tick-tick.

"Zern kaid-whit?" rasped the loudspeaker. *"Zern kaid-whit?"*

That was code and meant, "Identify yourself—friend or foe?"

Taking the pilot's seat, he turned a key that caused his transmitter to squirt forth a short and ultra-rapid series of numbers. Then he rubbed his eyes and looked into the forward starfield. Apart from the majestic haze of suns shining in the dark there was nothing to be seen with the naked eye.

So he switched on his thermosensitive detector screens

and was rewarded with a line of brilliant dots paralleling his course to starboard while a second group, in arrow formation, was about to cut across far ahead of his nose. He was not seeing the ships, of course, but only the visible evidence of their white-hot propulsion tubes and flaming tails.

"Keefa!" said the loudspeaker, meaning, "All correct!"

Crawling back into the bunk, Leeming hauled a blanket over his face, closed his eyes and left the autopilot to carry on. After ten minutes his mind began to drift into a pleasant, soothing dream about sleeping in free space with nobody to bother him.

Dropping its code-talk, the loudspeaker yelped in plain language, "Cut speed before we lose you."

He sat up as if stung, stared blearily across the cabin. Somebody had spoken, somebody with a parade-ground voice. Or had he imagined it? He waited a bit but nothing happened and so he lay down again.

The loudspeaker bawled impatiently, "You deaf? Cut speed before we lose you!"

Leeming clambered irefully from the bunk, sat at the controls, adjusted them slowly. A thin braking-jet in the bow let go a double plume of vapour that swept back on either side as the ship overtook and passed by. The stern tubes meanwhile decreased their thrust. He watched his meters until he thought their needles had dropped far enough to make the others happy. Then he returned to bed and hid himself under the blanket.

It seemed to him that he was swinging in a celestial hammock and enjoying a wonderful idleness when the loudspeaker roared, "Cut more! Cut more!"

He shot out from under the blanket, scrambled to the controls and cut more. Then he switched on his transmitter and made a speech distinguished by its passion. It was partly a seditious outburst and partly a lecture upon the basic functions of the human body. For all he knew the astonished listeners might include two rear-admirals and a dozen commodores. If so, he was educating them.

In return he received no heated retorts, no angry voice of authority. If he had broadcast the same words from a heavily manned battleship they'd have plastered him with forty charges and set the date for his court-martial. But it was space-navy convention that a lone scout's job created an unavoidable craziness among all those who performed it and that ninety per cent of them were overdue for psychiatric treatment. A scout on active service could and often did say things that nobody else in the space-navy dared utter. It is a wonderful thing to be recognised as dotty.

For three weeks they accompanied him in the glum silence with which a family takes around an imbecile relation. He chafed impatiently during this period because their top speed was far, far below his maximum velocity and the need to keep pace with them gave him the feeling of an urgent motorist trapped behind a funeral procession.

The Sirian battleship *Wassoon* was the chief culprit, a great, clumsy contraption that wallowed along like a bloated hippopotamus while a shoal of faster cruisers and destroyers were compelled to amble with it. He did not know its name but he did know that it was a battleship because on his detector screens it resembled a glowing pea amid an array of fiery pinheads. Every time he looked at the pea he cursed it something awful. He was again venting his ire upon it when the loudspeaker chipped in and spoke for the first time in many days.

"Ponk!"

Ponk? What the devil was ponk? The word meant something mighty important, he could remember that much. Hastily he scrabbled through the code-book and found it: *Enemy in sight*.

No sign of the foe was visible on his screens. Evidently they were beyond detector range and had been spotted only by the escort's advance-guard of four destroyers running far ahead.

"Dial F," ordered the loudspeaker.

So they were changing frequency in readiness for battle. Leeming turned the dial of his multiband receiver from T back to F. Laconic interfleet messages came through the speaker in a steady stream.

"Offside group port twenty, rising inclination twelve."

"Check!"

"Break off."

"Check!"

On the screens five glowing dots swiftly angled away from the main body of the escort. Four were mere pinheads, the fifth and middle one about half the size of the pea. A cruiser and four destroyers were escaping the combat area for the time-honoured purpose of getting between the enemy and his nearest base.

In a three-dimensional medium where speeds were tremendous and space was vast this tactic never worked. It did not stop both sides from trying to make it work whenever the opportunity came along. This could be viewed as eternal optimism or persistent stupidity, according to the state of one's liver.

The small group of would-be ambushers scooted as fast as they could make it, hoping to become lost within the confusing welter of starlights before the enemy came near enough to detect the move. Meanwhile the *Wassoon* and its attendant cohort plugged steadily onward. Ahead, almost at the limit of the fleet's detector range, the four destroyers continued to advance without attempting to disperse or change course.

"Two groups of ten converging from forty-five degrees rightward, descending inclination fifteen," reported the forward destroyers.

"Classification?" demanded the *Wassoon*.

"Not possible yet."

Silence for six hours, then, "Two groups still maintaining same course; each appears to consist of two heavy cruisers and eight monitors."

That was sheer guesswork based upon the theory that the greater the detectable heat the bigger the ship. Leeming watched his screens knowing full well that the enemy's vessels might prove to be warships as the observers supposed or might equally well turn out to be escorted convoys of merchantmen. Since the spatial war first broke out many a lumbering tramp had been mistaken for a monitor.

Slowly, ever so slowly, twenty faintly discernible dots bloomed into his screens. This was the time when he and his escort should be discovered by the enemy's detection devices. The foe must have spotted the leading destroyers hours ago; either they weren't worried about a mere four ships or, more likely, had taken it for granted that they were friendly. It would be interesting to watch their reaction when they found the strong force farther behind.

He did not get the chance to observe this pleasing phenomenon. The loudspeaker let go a squawk of, "Ware zenith!" and automatically his gaze jerked upward to the screens above his head. They were poxed with a host of rapidly enlarging dots. He estimated that sixty to eighty ships were diving in fast at ninety degrees to the plane of the escort, but he didn't stop to count them. One glance was sufficient to tell him that he was in a definite hot-spot.

Forthwith he lifted his slender vessel's nose and switched to full boost. The result pinned him in his seat while his intestines tried to wrap themselves around his spine. It was easy to imagine the effect upon the enemy's screens; they would see one mysterious, unidentifiable ship break loose from the target area and swoop around them at a speed previously thought impossible.

With luck, they might assume that what one ship could do all the others could do likewise. If there is anything a spaceship captain detests it is to have another and faster ship sneaking up on his tail. The fiery end of a spaceship is its weak spot for there can be no effective armament in an area filled with propulsors.

Stubbornly, Leeming stuck to the upward curve which, if maintained long enough, would take him well to one side of the approaching attackers and round to the back of them. He kept full attention upon his screens. The oncomers held course in a tight, vengeful knot for four hours, by which time they were almost within shooting range of the escort. At that point their nerve failed. The fact that the escort still kept impassive formation while one ship headed like a shooting star for their rear made them suspect a trap. One thing the Combine never lacked was suspicion of the Allies' motives and unshakable faith in their cunning.

So they curved out at right-angles and spread in all directions like the petals of a blown flower, their detectors probing for another and bigger fleet that might be lurking just beyond visibility.

Belting along at top pace, one Lathian light cruiser realized that its new course would bring it within range of the missiles with which Leeming's strange, superfast ship presumably was armed. It tried to play safe by changing course again and thereby delivered itself into the hands of the *Wassoon*'s electronic predictors. The *Wassoon* fired, its missiles met the cruiser at the precise point where it came within range. Cruiser and missiles tried to occupy the same space at the same time. The result was a soundless explosion of great magnitude and a flare of heat that temporarily obliterated every detector screen within reach.

Another blast shone briefly high in the starfield and far beyond reach of the escort's armaments. A few minutes later a thin, reedy voice, distorted by static, reported that a straggling enemy destroyer had fallen foul of the distant ambushing party. This sudden loss, right outside the scene of action, seemed to confirm the enemy's belief that the *Wassoon* and its attendant fleet might be mere bait in a trap loaded with something formidable. They continued to radiate fast from their common centre in an effort to locate the hidden menace and, at the same time, avoid being caught in a bunch.

Seeing them thus darting away like a shoal of frightened fish, Leeming muttered steadily to himself. A dispersed fleet should be easy prey to a superfast ship capable of overhauling and dealing with its units one by one. He had to face the fact that his vessel could do nothing more than scare them individually while he lavished futile curses upon them. Without a single effective weapon he was impotent to take advantage of an opportunity that might never occur again. For the moment he had quite forgotten his role, not to mention his strict orders to avoid a space-fight at all costs.

The *Wassoon* soon reminded him with a sharp call of, "Scout-pilot, where the hell d'you think you're going?"

"Up and around," replied Leeming sourly.

"You're more of a liability than an asset," retorted the *Wassoon*, unappreciative of his efforts. "Get out while the going is good."

Leeming yelled into the microphone, "I know when I'm not wanted, see? Spitting on parade is a punishable offence, see? Remember man, you must *always* salute a commodore. Stand properly to attention when you speak to me! We're being sabotaged by defective zippers. Come on, lift those feet Dopey—one, two, three, *hup!*"

As before, the listeners took no notice whatsoever. Leeming turned his ship on to a new course with plane parallel to that of the escort and high above them. They now became visible on his underbelly screens and showed themselves in the same unbroken formation but sweeping in a wide circle to get on the reverse course. That meant they were leaving him and heading homeward. The enemy, still scattered beyond shooting range, must have viewed this move as wicked temptation for although in superior strength they continued to refrain from direct attack.

Quickly the escort's array of shining dots slid off the screens as Leeming's vessel shot away from them. Ahead and well to starboard the detectors showed the two enemy groups that had first appeared. They had not dispersed in the same manner that their main force had done but their course showed that they were fleeing the area at the best pace they could muster. This fact suggested that they really were two convoys of merchantmen hugging close to their protecting cruisers. With deep regret Leeming watched them go. Given the weapons he could have swooped upon the bloated parade and slaughtered a couple of heavily-laden ships before the cruisers had time to wake up.

At full pelt he dived into the Combine's front and headed toward the unknown back areas. Just before his detectors lost range his tailward screen flared up twice in quick succession. Far behind him two ships had ceased to exist and there was no way of telling whether these losses had been suffered by the escort or the enemy.

He tried to find out by calling on the interfleet frequency, "What goes? What goes?"

No answer.

A third flash covered the screen. It was weak with distance and swiftly fading sensitivity.

Keying the transmitter to give his identifying codenumber, he called again.

No reply.

If the battle had joined far to his rear they'd be much too busy to bother with his queries. He'd have given a lot to turn back and see for himself what was happening, to join the hooley and help litter the cosmos with wreckage. But without a major or minor weapon he was precisely what the *Wassoon* had declared him to be, namely, an unmitigated nuisance.

Chewing his bottom lip with annoyance, he squatted four-square in the pilot's seat and scowled straight ahead while the ship arrowed toward a dark gap in the hostile starfield. In due time he got beyond the full limit of Allied warships' non-stop range. At that point he also got beyond help.

The first world was easy meat. Believing it impossible for any Allied ship to penetrate this far without refuelling and changing tubes, the enemy assumed that any ship detected in local space must be friendly or, at least, neutral. Therefore when picked up by their detectors they did not bother to radio a challenge and identify him as hostile by his inability to give a correct reply. They let him zoom around unhampered by official nosiness.

So he found the first occupied world by the simple process of shadowing a small convoy heading inward from the spatial front, following them long enough to make an accurate plot of their course. Then, because he could not afford to waste days and weeks crawling along at their relatively slow pace, he arced over them and raced ahead until he reached the inhabited planet for which they were bound.

Checking the planet was equally easy. He went twice around its equator at altitude sufficiently low to permit swift visual observation. Complete coverage of the sphere was not necessary to gain a shrewd idea of its status, development and potentialities. What he could see in a narrow strip around its belly was enough of a sampling for the purposes of the Terran Intelligence Service.

In short time he spotted three spaceports, two empty, the third holding eight merchant ships of unknown origin and three Combine war vessels. Other evidence showed the world to be heavily populated and well-advanced. He could safely mark it as a pro-Combine planet of considerable military value.

Shooting back into free space, he dialled X, the special long-range frequency, and beamed this information together with the planet's approximate diameter, mass and spatial co-ordinates.

"I dived in and circumnavigated the dump," he said, and let go a snigger. He couldn't help it because he was recalling his careless response to a similar situation set as a test-piece in his first examination.

He had written, "I made cautious approach to the strange planet and then quickly circumcised it."

The paper had come back marked, "Why?"

He'd replied, "I could get around better by taking short cuts."

It had cost him ten marks and the dead-pan comment, "This information lacks either accuracy or wit." But he had passed all the same.

There was no reply to his signal and he did not expect one. He could beam signals outward with impunity but they could not beam back into enemy territory without awakening hostile listening-posts to the fact that someone must be operating in their back areas. Beamed signals were highly directional and the enemy was always on the alert to pick up and decipher anything emanating from the Allied front while ignoring all broadcasts from the rear.

The next twelve worlds were found in substantially the same manner as the first one: by plotting interplanetary and interstellar shipping routes and following them to their termini. He signalled details of each one and each time was rewarded with silence. By this time he found himself deploring the necessary lack of response because he had been going long enough to yearn for the sound of a human voice.

After weeks that stretched to months, enclosed in a thundering metal bottle, he was becoming afflicted with an appalling loneliness. Amid this vast stretch of stars, with seemingly endless planets on which lived not a soul to call him Joe, he could have really enjoyed the arrival from faraway of an irate human voice bawling him out good and proper for some error, real or fancied. He'd have sat there and bathed his mind in the stream of abuse. Constant, never-ending silence was the worst of all, the hardest to bear.

Occasionally he tried to break the hex by singing at the top of his voice or by holding heated arguments with himself while the ship howled onward. It was a poor and ineffectual substitute because he was less musical than a tumescent tomcat and he couldn't win an argument without also losing it.

His sleeps were lousy, too. Sometimes he dreamed that the autopilot had gone haywire and that the ship was heading full-tilt into a blazing sun. Then he'd wake up with his belly jumping and make quick, anxious check of the apparatus before returning to slumber. Other times he awoke heavy-eyed and dry-mouthed feeling that he'd had no sleep at all, but had been lying supine through hours of constant trembling and a long, sustained roar.

Several times he had pursuit-dreams in which he was being chased through dark, metallic corridors that bellowed and quivered all around while close behind him sounded the rapid, vengeful tread of feet that were not feet. Invariably he woke up just as he was about to be grabbed by hands that were not hands.

In theory there was no need for him to suffer the wear and tear of long-range reconnaissance. A case full of wonder-drugs had been provided to cope with every conceivable condition of mind or body. The trouble was that they were effective or they were not. If ineffective, the taking of them proved sheer waste of time. If effective, they tended to shove things to the opposite extreme.

Before one sleep-period he had experimented by taking a so-called normalising capsule positively guaranteed to get rid of nightmares and ensure happy, interesting dreams. The result had been ten completely uninhibited hours in a harem. They had been hours so utterly interesting that they'd left him flat out. He never took another capsule.

It was while he was nosing after a merchant convoy, in expectation of tracing a thirteenth planet, that he got some vocal sounds that at least broke the monotony: He was following far behind and high above the group of ships and they, feeling secure in their own backyard, were keeping no detector-watch and were unaware of his presence. Fiddling idly with the controls of his receiver he suddenly hit upon an enemy interfleet frequency and picked up a conversation between ships.

The unknown lifeform manning the vessels had loud, somewhat bellicose voices but spoke a language with sound-forms curiously akin to Terran speech. To Leeming's ears it came as a stream of cross-talk that his mind instinctively framed in Terran words. It went like this:

First voice: "Mayor Snorkum will lay the cake."

Second voice: "What for the cake be laid by Snorkum?"

First voice: "He will starch his mustache."

Second voice: "That is night-gab. How can he starch a tepid mouse?"

They spent the next ten minutes in what sounded like an acrimonious argument about what one repeatedly called a tepid mouse while the other insisted that it was a torpid moose. Leeming found that trying to follow the point and counterpoint of this debate put quite a strain upon the cerebellum. He suffered it until something snapped.

Tuning his transmitter to the same frequency, he bawled, "Mouse or moose, make up your goddam minds!"

This produced a moment of dumbfounded silence before the first voice harshed, "Gnof, can you lap a pie-chain?"

"No, he can't," shouted Leeming, giving the unfortunate Gnof no chance to brag of his ability as a pie-chain lapper.

There came another pause, then Gnof resentfully told all and sundry, "I shall lambast my mother."

"Dirty dog!" said Leeming. "Shame on you!"

The other voice now informed, mysteriously, "Mine is a fat one."

"I can imagine," Leeming agreed.

"Clam-shack?" demanded Gnof in tones clearly translatable as, "Who is that?"

"Mayor Snorkum," Leeming told him.

For some weird reason known only to alien minds this information caused the argument to start all over again. They commenced by debating Mayor Snorkum's antecedents and future prospects (or so it sounded) and gradually and enthusiastically worked their way along to the tepid mouse (or torpid moose).

There were moments when they became mutually heated about something or other, possibly Snorkum's habit of keeping his moose on a pie-chain. Finally they dropped the subject by common consent and switched to the abstruse question of how to paddle a puddle (according to one) or how to peddle a poodle (according to the other).

"Holy cow!" said Leeming fervently.

It must have borne close resemblance to something pretty potent in the hearers' language because they broke off and again Gnof challenged, "Clam-shack?"

"Go jump, Buster!" Leeming invited.

"Bosta? My ham-plank is Bosta, *enk*?" His tones suggested considerable passion about the matter as he repeated, "Bosta, *enk*?"

"Yeah," confirmed Leeming. *"Enk!"*

Apparently this was regarded as the last straw for their voices went off and even the faint hum of the carrier-wave disappeared. It looked as though he had managed to utter something extremely vulgar without having the vaguest notion of what he had said.

Soon afterward the carrier-wave came on and another and different voice called in guttural but fluent Cosmoglotta, "What ship? What ship?"

Leeming did not answer.

A long wait before again the voice demanded, "What ship?"

Still Leeming took no notice. The mere fact that they had not broadcast a challenge in war-code showed that they did not believe it possible for a hostile vessel to be in the vicinity. Indeed, this was suggested by the stolid way in which the convoy continued to plug along without changing course or showing visible sign of alarm.

It was highly likely that they could not so much as see his ship, not being equipped with sufficiently sensitive detectors. The call of, "What ship?" had been nothing more than a random feel in the dark, an effort to check up before seeking a practical joker somewhere within the convoy itself.

Having obtained adequate data on the enemy's course, Leeming bulleted ahead of them and in due time came across the thirteenth planet. He beamed the information homeward, went in search of the next. It was found quickly, being in an adjacent solar system

Time rolled by as his probes took him across a broad stretch of Combine-controlled space and measured its precise depth. After discovering the fiftieth planet he was tempted to return to base for overhaul and further orders. One can have a surfeit of exploration and he was sorely in need of a taste of Terra, its fresh air, green fields, and human companionship.

What kept him going were the facts that the ship was running well, his fuel supply was only a quarter expended, and he could not resist the notion that the more thoroughly he did this job the greater the triumph upon his return and the better the prospect of quick promotion.

So on he went and piled up the total to seventy-two planets before he reached a preselected point where he was deep in the enemy hinterland at a part facing the Allied outposts around Rigel. From here he was expected to send a coded signal to which they would respond, this being the only message they'd risk sending him.

He beamed the one word, "Awa!" repeated at intervals for a couple of hours. It meant, "Able to proceed—awaiting instructions." To that they should give a reply too brief for enemy interceptors to catch; either the word, "Reeter!" meaning "We have sufficient information—return at once," or else the word, "Buzz" meaning "We need more information—continue your reconnaissance."

What he did get back was a short-short squirt of sound that he recognised as an ultra-rapid series of numbers. They came in so fast that it was impossible to note them aurally. Perforce he taped them as they were repeated, then reached for his code-book as he played them off slowly.

The result was, "47926 Scout-Pilot John Leeming promoted Lieutenant as from date of receipt."

He stared at this a long time before he resumed sending, "Awa! Awa!" For his pains he got back the word, "Foit!" He tried again and once more was rewarded with, "Foit!" It looked vaguely blasphemous to him, like the favourite curse of some rubbery creature that had no palate.

Irritated by this piece of nonsense, he stewed it over in his mind, decided that some intervening Combine station was playing his own game by chipping in with confusing comments. In theory the enemy shouldn't be able to do it because he was using a frequency far higher than those favoured by the Lathians and others, while both his and the Allied messages were scrambled. All the same, *somebody* was doing it.

To the faraway listeners near Rigel he beamed the interesting biological statement that Mayor Snorkum would lay the moose and left them to sort it out for themselves. Maybe it would teach some nuthead that he was now dealing with a full lieutenant and not a mere scout-pilot. Or, if the enemy intercepted it, they could drop their war-effort while they argued their way around to a final and satisfactory peddling of the poodle.

Concluding that no recall meant the same thing as not being recalled, he resumed his search for hostile planets. It was four days later that he happened to be looking idly through his code-book and found the word, "Foit" defined as "Use your own judgment."

He thought it over, decided that to go home with a record of seventy-two planets discovered and identified would be a wonderful thing, but to be credited with a nice, round, imposing number such as one hundred would be wonderful enough to verge upon the miraculous. They'd make him a Space Admiral at least. He'd be able to tell Colonel Farmer to get a haircut and order Commodore Keen to polish his buttons. He could strut around clanking with medals and be a saint to all the privates and spacecadets, a swine to all the brasshats.

This absurd picture was so appealing that he at once settled for a score of one hundred planets as his target-figure before returning to base. As if to give him the flavour of coming glory, four enemy-held worlds were found close together in the next solar system and these boosted his total to seventy-six.

He shoved the score up to eighty. Then to eighty-one.

The first hint of impending disaster showed itself as he approached number eighty-two.

Chapter 3

Two dots glowed in his detector-screens. They were fat but slow-moving and it was impossible to decide whether they were warships or cargo-boats. But they were travelling in line abreast and obviously headed someplace to which he'd not yet been. Using his always successful tactics of shadowing them until he had obtained a plot, he followed them awhile, made sure of the star toward which they were heading and then bolted onward.

He had got so far in advance that the two ships had faded right out of his screens when suddenly a propulsor-tube blew its dessicated lining forty miles back along the jet-track. The first he knew of it was when the alarm-bell shrilled on the instrument-board, the needle of the pressure meter dropped halfway back, the needle of its companion heat meter crawled toward the red dot that indicated melting-point.

Swiftly he cut off the feed to that propulsor. Its pressure

meter immediately fell to zero, its heat meter climbed a few more degrees, hesitated, stayed put a short while then reluctantly slid back.

The ship's tail fin was filled with twenty huge propulsors around which were splayed eight steering jets of comparatively small diameter. If any one propulsor ceased to function the effect was not serious. It meant no more than a five per cent loss in power output and a corresponding loss in the ship's functional efficiency. On Earth they had told him that he could sacrifice as many as eight propulsors—providing that they were symetrically positioned—before his speed and manoeuvrability were reduced to those of a Combine destroyer.

From the viewpoint of his technical advantage over the foe he had nothing to worry about—yet. He could still move fast enough to make them look like spatial sluggards. What *was* worrying was the fact that the sudden breakdown of the refractory lining of one main driver might be forewarning of the general condition of the rest. For all he knew, another propulsor might go haywire any minute and be followed by the remainder in rapid succession.

Deep inside him was the feeling that now was the time to turn back and make for home while the going was good. Equally deep was the hunch that he'd never get there because already he had travelled too long and too far. The ship was doomed never to see Earth again; inwardly he was as sure of that as one can be sure of anything.

But the end of the ship need not mean the end of its pilot even though he be wandering like a lost soul through strange areas of a hostile starfield. The precognition that told Leeming his ship was heading for its grave also assured him that he was not. He felt it in his bones that the day was yet to come when, figuratively speaking, he would blow his nose in Colonel Farmer's handkerchief.

Rejecting the impulse to reverse course and run for Rigel, he kept stubbornly on toward planet number eighty-two, reached it, surveyed it and beamed the information. Then he detected a shipping route between here and a nearby solar system, started along it in the hope of finding planet number eighty-three and adding it to his score. A second propulsor shed its lining when halfway there, a third just before arrival.

All the same, he circumnavigated the world at reduced speed, headed for free space with the intention of transmitting the data but never did so. Five more propulsors blew their linings simultaneously. He had to move mighty fast to cut off the feed before their unhampered blasts could melt his entire tail away.

The defective drivers must have been bunched together off-centre for the ship now refused to run straight. Instead it started to describe a wide curve that eventually would bring it back in a great circle to the planet it had just left. To make matters worse, it also commenced a slow, regular rotation around its longitudinal axis with the result that the entire starfield seemed to revolve before Leeming's eyes.

Desperately he tried to straighten the ship's course by means of the steering jets but this only produced an eerie swaying which, combined with the rotation, caused his fire-trail to shape itself into an elongated spiral. The curve continued until planet eighty-three slid into one side of his observation port and spun slowly around it. Two more propulsors blew long, thin clouds of ceramic dust far backward. The planet swelled enormously in the armourglass. Yet another propulsor gave up the ghost.

The vessel was now beyond all hope of salvation as a cosmos-traversing vehicle and the best he could hope to do with it was to get it down in one piece for the sake of his own skin. He concentrated solely upon achieving this end. Though in serious condition the ship was not wholly beyond control because the steering jets could function perfectly when not countered by a lopsided drive, while the braking jets were capable of roaring with full-throated power.

As the planet filled the forward view and its crinkled surface expanded into hills and valleys, he cut off all remaining tail propulsors, used his steering jets to hold the ship straight and blew his braking jets repeatedly. The longitudinal rotation ceased and speed of descent slowed while his hands sweated at the controls.

It was dead certain that he could not land in the orthodox manner by standing the ship on its tail-fins. He lacked enough power-output to come down atop a carefully-controlled column of fire. The ship was suffering from a much-dreaded condition known to the space service as weak-arse and that meant he'd have to make a belly landing at just enough speed to retain control up to the last moment.

His eyes strained at the observation port while the oncoming hills widened, the valleys lengthened and the planet's surface fuzz changed to a pattern of massed treetops. Then the whole picture appeared to leap at him as if suddenly brought into focus under a powerful microscope. He fired four propulsors and the lower steering jets in an effort to level-off.

The nose lifted as the vessel shot across a valley and cleared the opposite hill by a few hundred feet. In the next two minutes he saw five miles of tree-tops, a clearing from which arose an army of trellis masts bearing radio antennas, a large village standing beside a river, another great expanse of trees followed by a gently rolling stretch of moorland.

This was the place! Mentally offering a quick prayer to

God, he swooped in a shallow curve with all braking jets going full blast. Despite this dexterous handling the first contact slung him clean out of his seat and threw him against the metal wall beneath his bunk. Bruised and shaken but otherwise unhurt, he scrambled from under the bunk while still the ship slid forward to the accompaniment of scraping, knocking sounds from under its belly.

Gaining the control-board, he stopped the braking jets, cut off all power. A moment later the vessel expended the last of its forward momentum and came to a halt. The resulting silence was like nothing he had experienced in many months. It seemed almost to bang against his ears. Each breath he took became a loud hiss, each step a noisy, metallic clank.

Going to the lock, he examined the atmospheric analyser. It registered exterior air pressure at fifteen pounds and said that it was much like Terra's except that it was slightly richer in oxygen. At once he went through the air-lock, stood in the rim of its outer door and found himself fourteen feet above ground-level.

The automatic ladder was of no use in this predicament since it was constructed to extend itself from air-lock to tail, a direction that now was horizontal. He could hang by his hands from the rim and let himself drop without risk of injury but he could not jump fourteen feet to get back in. The one thing he lacked was a length of rope.

"They think of everything," he complained, talking out loud because a justifiable gripe deserves to be uttered. "They think of everything imaginable. Therefore twenty feet of rope is not imaginable. Therefore I can imagine the unimaginable. Therefore I am cracked. Anyone who talks to himself is cracked. It's legitimate for a looney to say what he likes. When I get back I'll say what I like and it'll be plenty!"

Feeling a bit better for that he returned to the cabin, hunted in vain for something that would serve in lieu of rope. He was about to rip his blankets into suitable strips when he remembered the power cables snaking from control-board to engine-room. It took him a hurried half hour to detach a suitable length from its terminals and tear it from its wall fastenings.

During the whole of this time his nerves were tense and his ears were continually perked for outside sounds indicating the approach of the enemy. If they should arrive in time to trap him within the ship he'd have no choice but to set off the explosive charge and blow himself apart along with the vessel. It was of major importance that the ship should not fall intact into alien hands and his own life was a secondary consideration.

Naturally he was most reluctant to spread himself in bloody shreds over the landscape and therefore moved fast with jumpy nerves, taut mind and stretched ears. Silence was still supreme when he tied one end of the cable inside the lock, tossed the rest outside and slid down it to ground.

He landed in thick, cushiony vegetation bearing slight resemblance to heather. Racing to the ship's tail, he had a look at the array of propulsors, realised that he was lucky to have survived. Eleven of the great tubes were completely without their essential linings, the remaining nine were in poor condition and obviously could not have withstood more than another two or three days of steady blasting.

It was out of the question to effect any repairs or even to take the ship up again for a short hop to somewhere more secluded. The long, sleek boat had set up an all-time record by bearing him safely through a good slice of the galaxy, past strange suns and around unknown worlds, and now it was finished. He could not help feeling mournful about it.

To destroy such a ship would be like cold-blooded murder—but it had to be done.

Now he took a quick look at what was visible of the world on which he stood. The sky was a deep, dark blue verging obscurely to purple, with a faint, cloudlike haze on the eastern horizon. The sun, now past its zenith, looked a fraction larger than Sol, had a redder colour, and its rays produced a slight and not unpleasant stinging sensation.

Underfoot the heather-like growth covered a gently undulating landscape running to the eastward horizon where the first ranks of trees stood guard. Through it, an immense scar ran the long, deep rut caused by the ship's belly-skid. To the west the undergrowth again gave way to great trees, the edge of the forest being half a mile away.

Leeming now found himself in another quandary of the kind not foreseen by those unable to imagine a need for rope. If he blew the ship to pieces he would destroy with it a lot of stuff he needed now or might need later on, in particular a large stock of concentrated food. To save the latter he would have to remove it from the ship, take it a safe distance from the coming explosion and hide it someplace where enemy patrols would not find it.

The nearby forest was the ideal place for a cache. But to salvage everything worth having he'd have to make several trips into the forest and risk the enemy putting in an appearance when he was too far from the ship to regain it ahead of them and set off the big bang.

If he became a wandering fugitive, as he intended, it was possible that he'd have no trouble finding enough food to keep him going for years. But he could not be sure of that. He knew nothing about this world except that it held intelligent life and was part of or in cahoots with the Combine. He couldn't so much as guess what its native lifeform looked like though it was a pretty safe bet that—like every other known sentient form—it was more or less humanoid.

Sense of urgency prevented him from pondering the situation very long. This was a time for action rather than thought. He started working like a maniac, grabbing packages and cans from the ship's store and throwing them out of the air-lock. This went on until the entire food stock had been cleared. Still the enemy was conspicuous by his absence.

Now he took up armloads from the waiting pile and bore them into the edge of the forest. Sheer anxiety made him waste a lot of effort for at each trip he tried to take more than he could hold. His route into the forest was marked back by dropped cans that had to be picked up at each return to the ship. These returns he made at the run, pausing only to snatch up the fallen stuff, and arriving breathless and already half-loaded.

By dint of haste and perspiration he transferred all the foodstuffs into the forest, climbed aboard the ship, had a last look around for anything worth saving. Making a roll of his blankets, he tied a waterproof sheet over them to form a compact bundle.

Regretfully he eyed the radio transmitter. It would be easy to send out a signal saying that he was marooned on planet number eighty-three and giving its co-ordinates. But it would not do him any good. No Allied vessel other than a special scout-ship could hope to get this far without refueling and having its tubes relined. Even if a ship did manage to cover the distance non-stop it stood little chance of finding and picking up one lone Terran hiding on a hostile world.

Satisfied that nothing remained worth taking, he put on his storm-coat, tucked the bundle under his arm and pressed the red button at one side of the control-board. There was supposed to be a delay of two minutes between activation and the resulting wallop. It wasn't much time. Bolting through the air-lock, he jumped straight out, landed heavily in the cushion of vegetation and dashed at top speed toward the forest. Nothing had happened by the time he reached the trees. Standing behind the protective thickness of a great trunk, he waited for the bang.

Seconds ticked by without results. Something must have gone wrong. Perhaps those who could not imagine rope could not think of a fuse or detonator either. He peeked cautiously around the rim of the trunk, debating within himself whether to go back and examine the connections to the explosive charge. At that point the ship blew up.

It flew apart with a tremendous, ear-splitting roar that bent the trees and shook the skies. A great column of smoke, dirt and shapeless lumps soared to a considerable height. Gobs of distorted metal screamed through the treetops and brought branches crashing down. A blast of hot wind rushed either side of the trunk behind which Leeming was sheltering, for a moment created a partial vacuum that made him gasp for breath.

Then followed a pattering sound like that of heavy rain, also many loud thumps as soil and scrap metal fell back to earth. Somewhat awed by the unexpected violence of the explosion, he sneaked another look around the tree-trunk, saw a smoking crater surrounded by two or three acres of torn vegetation. It was a sobering thought that for countless millions of miles he had been sitting on top of a bang that size.

When tardily the foe arrived it was pretty certain that they would start a hunt for the missing crew. Leeming's preliminary survey of the world, though consisting only of one quick sweep around its equator, had found evidence of some sort of organised civilisation and included one space-

41

port holding five merchant ships and one Combine light cruiser, all of antiquated pattern. This showed that the local lifeform was at least of normal intelligence and as capable as anyone else of adding two and two together.

The relative shallowness of the crater and the wide scattering of remnants was clear evidence that the mystery ship had not plunged to destruction but rather had blown apart after making a successful landing. Natives in the nearest village could confirm that there had been quite a long delay between the ship's plunge over their rooftops and the subsequent explosion. The foe would know that none of his own ships were missing in that area. Examination of fragments would reveal non-Combine material. Their inevitable conclusion: that the vessel had been a hostile one and that its crew had got away unscathed.

It would be wise, he decided, to put more distance between himself and the crater before the enemy arrived and started sniffing around the vicinity. Perhaps he was fated to be caught eventually but it was up to him to postpone the evil day as long as possible.

The basic necessities of life are food, drink and shelter, with the main emphasis on the first of these. This fact delayed his departure a little while. He had food enough to last for several months. It was one thing to have it, another to keep it safe from harm. At all costs he must find a better hiding place to which he could return from time to time with the assurance that the supply would still be there.

He pressed farther into the forest, moving in a wide zigzag as he cast about for a suitable dump. Visibility was good because the sun remained high and the trees did not entirely obscure the overhead view. He sought here and there, muttering angrily to himself and making vulgar remarks about officials who decided what equipment a scout-ship should carry. If he'd had a spade he could have dug a neat hole and buried the stuff. But he did not have a spade and it would take too long to scrabble a hideout with his bare hands.

Finally he found a cave-like opening between the great arched roots of an immense tree. It was far from ideal but it did have the virtue of being deep within the woods and providing a certain amount of concealment. Casting around, he picked up a smooth, heavy pebble, flung it through the opening with all the force he could muster. There came no answering yelp, howl or squeal, no sudden rush of some outlandish creature intent on mayhem. The cave was unoccupied.

It took him more than an hour to shift the food-pile for the third time and stack it neatly within the hole, leaving out a small quantity representing seven days' rations. When this task had been completed he built up part of the opening with clumps of earth, used twigs and branches to fill in the rest. He now felt that if a regiment of enemy troops explored the locality, as they were likely to do, there was small chance of them discovering and either confiscating or destroying the cache on which his continued liberty might depend.

Stuffing the seven days' rations into a small rucksack and tying the bundled blankets thereto, he set off at fast pace along the fringe of the forest and headed southward. Right now he had no plan in mind, no especial purpose other than that of evading capture by making distance before the foe found the crater and searched the vicinity. He doubted whether the enemy would maintain such a local hunt for more than a couple of days after which they'd decide that there were no survivors or, alternatively, that it was high time that they started seeking them farther afield. Therefore it should be reasonably safe for him to return for food in about one week's time.

He had been going three hours and had covered eleven miles before the enemy showed the first signs of activity. With the moorland on his right and the forest on his left, he was trudging along when a black dot soared above the horizon, swelled in size, shot silently overhead and was followed some seconds later by a shrill scream.

Going at that height and at that speed the jetplane's pilot could not possibly have seen him. Unperturbed, he stepped into the shadow of a tree, turned to watch the machine as it diminished northward. It was again a mere dot when suddenly it swept around in a wide circle, spiralled upward and continued circling. As nearly as Leeming could judge it was turning high above the crater.

It was an easy guess that the jetplane had come in response to a telephone or radio call telling about a spaceship in distress and a following explosion. Having found the scene of disaster it was zooming above the spot while summoning help. No doubt there'd be great activity at the base from which it had come; receiving confirmation that a ship had indeed been lost, the authorities would assume it to be one of their own and start checking by radio to find which one was missing. With luck it might be quite a time before they accepted the fact that a vessel of unknown origin, probably hostile, had reached this far.

In any case, from now on they'd keep a sharp watch for survivors. Leeming decided that this was the time to leave the forest's fringe and progress under cover. His rate of movement would be slowed but at least he'd travel unobserved. There were two dangers in taking to the woods but they'd have to be accepted as lesser evils.

For one, unless he was mighty careful he could lose his

sense of direction and wander in a huge curve that eventually would take him back to the crater and straight into the arms of whoever was waiting there. For another, he ran the risk of encountering unknown forms of wild life possessed of unimaginable weapons and unthinkable appetites.

Against the latter peril he had a defence that was extremely effective but hateful to use, namely a powerful compressed-air pistol that fired breakable pellets filled with a stench so foul that one whiff would make anything that lived and breathed vomit for hours—including, as often as not, the user.

Some Terran genius had worked it out that the real king of the wilds is not the lion nor the grizzly bear but a kittenish creature named Joe Skunk whose every battle was a victorious rearguard action, so to speak. Some other genius had synthesized a horrible liquid seventy-seven times more revolting than Joe's—with the result that an endangered spaceman could never make up his mind whether to run like hell and chance being caught or whether to stand firm, shoot and subsequently puke himself to death.

Freedom is worth a host of risks, so he plunged deep into the forest and kept going. After about an hour's steady progress he heard the *whup-whup* of many helicopters passing overhead and travelling toward the north. By the sound of it there were quite a lot of them but none could be seen crossing the few patches of sky visible between the tree-tops.

He made a guess that they were a squadron of troop carriers transporting a search party to the region of the crater. Sometime later a solitary machine crept above with a loud humming noise while a downward blast of air made the trees rustle and wave their topmost branches. It was low and slow-moving and sounded like a buoyant fan that probably was carrying one observer. He stopped close by a gnarly trunk until it had passed.

Soon afterward he began to feel tired and decided to rest awhile upon a mossy bank. Reposing at ease, he pondered this exhaustion, realised that although his survey had shown this world to be approximately the same size as Terra it must in fact be a little bigger or had slightly greater mass. His own weight was up perhaps by as much as ten per cent, though he had no way of checking it.

True, after a long period of incarceration in a ship he must be out of condition but he was making full allowance for that fact. He was undoubtedly heavier than he'd been since birth, the rucksack was heavier, so were the blankets, so were his feet. Therefore his ability to cover mileage would be cut down in proportion and, in any emergency, so would his ability to run.

It then struck him that the day must be considerably longer than Earth's. The sinking sun was now about forty degrees above the horizon. In the time since he'd landed the arc it had covered showed that the day was somewhere between thirty and thirty-two hours in length. He'd have to accommodate himself to that with extended walks and prolonged sleeps and it wouldn't be easy. Wherever they may be, Terrans have a natural tendency to retain their own time-habits.

Isolation in space is a hell of a thing, he thought, as idly he toyed with the flat, oblong-shaped lump under the left-hand pocket of his jacket. The lump had been there so long that he was only dimly conscious of its existence and, even when reminded of it, tended to suppose that all jackets were made lumpy for some perverse reason known only to members of the International Garment Workers' Union. Now it struck him with what approximated to a flash of pure genius that in the long, long ago someone had once mentioned his lump and described it as "the built-in emergency-pack."

Taking out his pocket-knife, he used its point to unpick the lining of his jacket. This produced a flat, shallow box of brown plastic. A hair-thin line ran around its rim but there was no button, keyhole, grip or any other visible means of opening it. Pulling and pushing it in a dozen different ways had no effect whatever. He tried to insert the knife-blade in the hairline and pry the whole thing open; that failed and the knife slipped and he nicked his thumb. Sucking the thumb, he shoved his other hand through the slit lining and felt all around his jacket in the hope of discovering written instructions of some sort. All he got for his pains was fluff in his fingernails.

Reciting several of the nine million names of God, he kicked the box with aggravated vim. Either the kick was the officially approved method of dealing with it or some of the names were potent, for the box snapped open. At once he commenced examining the contents which, in theory, should assist him toward ultimate salvation.

The first was a tiny, bead-sized vial of transparent plastic ornamented with an embossed skull and containing an oily, yellowish liquid. Presumably this was the death-pill to be taken as a last extreme. Apart from the skull there was nothing to distinguish it from a love-potion.

Next came a long, thin bottle filled with what looked like diluted mud and marked with a long, imposing list of vitamins, proteins and trace elements. What one took it for, how much was supposed to be taken at a time, and how often, were left to the judgment of the beneficiary—or the victim.

After this came a small sealed can bearing no identifying

markings and devoid of a can-opener to go with it. For all he knew it might be full of boot polish, sockeye salmon or putty. He wouldn't put it past them to thoughtfully provide some putty in case he wanted to fix a window someplace and thus save his life by ingratiating himself with his captors. If, back home, some genius got it into his head that no lifeform known or unknown could possibly murder a window-fixer, a can of putty automatically became a must.

Dumping it at one side, he took up the next can. This was longer, narrower and had a rotatable cap. He twisted the cap and uncovered a sprinkler. Shaking it over his open palm he got a puff of fine powder resembling pepper. Well, that would come in very useful for coping with a pack of bloodhounds, assuming that there were bloodhounds in these here parts. Cautiously he sniffed at his palm. The stuff smelled exactly like pepper.

He let go a violent sneeze, wiped his dusty hand on a handkerchief, closed the can and concocted some heated remarks about the people at the space-base. This had immediate effect for the handkerchief burst into flames in his pocket. He tore it out, flung it down and danced on it. Opening the can again, he let a few grains of pepper fall upon a dry piece of rotten wood. A minute later the wood spat sparks and started blazing. This sent a betraying column of smoke skyward, so he danced on the wood until it ceased.

Exhibit number five really did explain itself—providing that its owner had the power of long-range clairvoyance. It was a tiny bottle of colourless liquid around which was wrapped a paper that said, "Administer two drops per hundred pounds bulk only in a non-carbonaceous beverage." A skull complete with crossbones added a sinister touch to this mysterious injunction.

After studying it for some time Leeming decided that the

liquid was either a poison or the knock-out additive favoured by Mr. Michael Finn. Apparently, if one were to encounter a twenty-ton rhinoceros the correct technique was to weigh it upon the nearest weighing-machine, calculate the appropriate dosage and administer it to the unfortunate animal in a non-carbonaceous beverage. One would then be safe because the creature would drop dead or fall asleep and lie with its legs in the air.

Number six was a miniature camera small enough to be concealed in the palm of the hand. As an aid to survival its value was nil. It must have been included in the kit with some other intention. Perhaps Terran Intelligence had insisted that it be provided in the hope that anyone who made successful escape from a hostile world could bring a lot of photographic data home with him. Well, it was nice to think that someone could be *that* optimistic. He pocketed the camera, not with any expectation of using it, but solely because it was a beautiful piece of microscopic workmanship too good to be thrown away.

The seventh and last was the most welcome and, so far as he was concerned, the only item worth a hoot; a luminous compass. He put it carefully into a vest pocket. After some consideration he decided to keep the pepper-pot but discarded the remaining cans and bottles. The death-pill he flicked into an adjacent bush. The bottles he shied between the trees. Finally he took the can of boot polish, sockeye, putty or whatever and hurled it as far as he could.

The result was a tremendous crash, a roar of flame and a large tree leaped twenty feet into the air with dirt showering from its roots. The blast knocked him full length on the moss; he picked himself up in time to see a great spurt of smoke sticking out of the tree-tops like a beckoning finger. Obviously visible for miles, it could not have been more effective if he'd sent up a balloon-borne banner bearing the words, "Here I am!"

Only one thing could be done and that was to get out fast. Grabbing up his load he scooted southward at the best pace he could make between the trees. He had covered about two miles when the buoyant fan hummed low down and slightly to his rear. A little later he heard the distant, muted *whup-whup* of a helicopter descending upon the scene of the crime. There'd be plenty of room for it to drop into the forest because the explosive can of something-or-other had cleared a wide gap. He tried to increase his speed, dodging around bushes, clambering up sharply sloping banks, jumping across deep, ditchlike depressions and all the time moving on leaden feet that felt as if he was wearing size twenty boots.

As the sun sank low and shadows lengthened he was again forced to rest through sheer exhaustion. By now he had no idea of the total distance covered; it had been impossible to travel in a dead straight line and the constant zig-zagging between the trees made mileage impossible to estimate. However, there were now no sounds of aerial activity either near or far away and, for all the evidence of the presence of other life, he might have the entire cosmos to himself.

Recovering, he pushed on until darkness was relieved only by the sparkle of countless stars and the shine of two small moons. Then he had a meal and bedded down in a secluded glade, rolling the blankets tightly around him and keeping his stink-gun near to hand. What kind of dangerous animal might stalk through the night he did not know and was long past caring. A man must have sleep come what may, even at the risk of waking up in somebody's belly.

Chapter 4

Lulled by the silence and his own tiredness, he slept for twelve hours. It was not an undisturbed slumber. Twice he awoke with the vague feeling that something had slunk past him in the dark. He lay completely still, nerves tense, gun in hand, his eyes straining to probe the surrounding gloom until at last sleep claimed him again, the eyelids fluttered and closed, he let go a subdued snore. Another time he awakened to see five moons in the sky, including a tiny, fast-moving one that arced across the vault of the heavens with a faint but hearable hiss. The vision was so brief and abnormal that for some time he was not sure whether he had actually witnessed it or merely dreamed it.

Despite the long and satisfying snooze he was only partway through the alien night. There were many hours to go before sunrise. Feeling refreshed and becoming bored by waiting, he gave way to his fidgets, rolled his blankets, consulted the compass and tried to continue his southward march. In short time he had tripped headlong over unseeable roots, stumbled knee-deep into a hidden stream.

Progress in open country was possible in the combined light of stars and moons, but not within the forest. Reluctantly he gave up the attempt. There was no point in wearing himself out blundering around in barely visible patches that alternated with areas of stygian darkness. Somehow he managed to find the glade again. There he lay in the blankets and waited with some impatience for the delayed dawn.

As the first faint glow appeared at one side of the sky something passed between the trees a hundred yards away. He got to his feet, gun pointing in that direction, watching and listening. Bushes rustled, dead leaves crackled and twigs snapped over a distance stretching from his left to far to his right.

The rate of motion was slow, laborious and the sounds suggested that the cause was sluggish and very heavy. Seeing nothing, he was unable to determine whether the noise was created by a troop of things crawling one behind the other or by one monstrous lifeform resembling a colossal worm, the grandpappy of all anacondas. Whatever it was, it did not come near to him and gradually the sounds died away.

Immediately daylight had become sufficiently strong to permit progress he resumed his southward trek and kept it up until mid-day. At that point he found a big rocky hollow that looked very much like an abandoned quarry. Trees grew thickly around its rim, bushes and lesser growths covered its floor, various kinds of creepers straggled down its walls. A tiny spring fed a midget stream that meandered across the floor until it disappeared down a hole in the base-rock. At least six caves were half-hidden in the walls, these varying from a narrow cleft to an opening the size of a large room.

Surveying the place, he realised that here was an ideal hideout. He had no thought of settling there for the rest of his natural life even if the availability of food permitted him to do so. He'd get nowhere by sitting on his quoit until he was old and rheumy. Besides, he'd had enough of a hermit's life in space without suffering more of it on firm land. But at least this locale would serve as a hiding-place until the hue and cry died down and he'd had time to think out his future plan of action.

Climbing down the steep, almost vertical sides to the floor of the place proved a tough task. From his viewpoint this was so much the better; whatever was difficult for him would be equally difficult for others and might deter any searching patrols that came snooping around. With that complete absence of logic that afflicts one at times, it didn't occur to him that a helicopter could come down upon him with no trouble at all.

He soon found a suitable cave and settled himself in by dumping his load on the dry, sandy ground. The next job was that of preparing a meal. Building a smokeless fire of wood chips, he filled his dixie with water and converted part of his rations into a thick soup. This, with some enriched wholemeal flatcakes, served to fill his belly and bring on a sense of peaceful wellbeing.

For a while he mooched around his sunken domain which covered four acres. The surrounding walls were eighty feet high while the crest of trees towered another two hundred feet higher. A scout-ship could have landed tail-first in this area and remained concealed for years from all eyes save those directly above. He found himself regretting that he had not known of this place and attempted an orthodox landing within it. Even if the ship toppled over through lack of adequate power, and he survived uninjured, he'd have the use of it as a permanent home and, if necessary, a fortress. Wouldn't be easy for the foe to winkle a man out of a heavy metal shell particularly when the said shell has fore and aft jets as effective as several batteries of guns.

Here and there were small holes in the ground. Similar holes were in evidence at the base of the walls. They reminded him of rabbit burrows. If whatever had made them was the alien equivalent of the rabbit it would be a welcome addition to his larder.

Getting down in crawling position, he peered into several of these apertures but could see nothing. He found a long, thin stick and poked it down some of them, without result. Finally he sat silent and motionless outside an array of holes for nearly two hours. At the end of that time a creature came out, saw him immediately and bolted back in. It resembled a fat and furry spider. Perhaps it was edible but the thought of eating it turned his stomach.

It then struck him that despite this planet's profuse supply of trees he had not seen or heard anything resembling a bird. If any arboreal creatures existed they must be in small number, or not native to this locality, or wholly nocturnal. There was also a noteworthy lack of insects and for this he was thankful. On any alien world the insect type of life could be and often was a major menace to any wandering Terran. That weird world of Hypatia, for instance, held streamlined whizz-bugs capable of travelling at six hundred miles per hour. A whizz-bug could drill a hole through a human being, space-suit and all, as neatly and effectively as a .45 slug.

At one end of the area grew a thick patch of feathery plants somewhat like giant ferns. They exuded a pleasantly aromatic scent. He gathered a good supply of these, laid them at the back of the cave, spread his blankets over them and thus made himself a bed more springy and comfortable than any he had enjoyed since childhood.

Although he had done everything in the most lackadaisical, time-wasting manner of which he was capable he still found it well-nigh impossible to cope with the lengthy day. He'd explored the pseudo-quarry from side to side, from one end to the other, had two meals, tidied the cave, done various chores necessary and unnecessary, and still the sun was far from setting. As nearly as he could calculate it would be another six hours before darkness fell. There was nothing to stop him from going to bed at the first yawn but if he did he'd surely wake up and face an equally long night. Adjustment to alien time did not come easy.

So he sat at the entrance to his cave and amused himself working out what best to do in the future. For a start, he could spend a couple of weeks transferring his foodstock from its place of concealment near the crater to this cave. Then, using his present headquarters as a strategic centre, he could make systematic exploration in all directions and get to know as much as possible about the potentialities of this world.

If investigation proved it possible to live off the land he could then travel farther afield, scout warily around inhabited areas until eventually he found a spaceport. Sooner or later the opportunity might come to sneak aboard a fully fuelled enemy scout-ship after dark and take it up with a triumphant bang. It was only one chance in a thousand, perhaps one in ten thousand, but it might come off. Yes, he'd go seeking such a chance and *make* it come off.

Even if he did manage to blast free in a Combine scout his problem would not be solved. No vessel could reach the Rigellian sector non-stop from here without at least one refuelling and one overhaul of propulsor tubes. To reach the

Allied front he'd have to break his journey partway there and repeat his present performance by dumping the ship and stealing another. What can be done once can be done twice. All the same, the odds against him ever seeing Terra were so tremendous that he did not care to think of them. He concentrated solely upon the ages-old thesis that while there's life there's hope.

Shortly before dusk a jetplane screamed across the sky as if to remind him that this world really was inhabited by superior life. Up to then the perpetual silence and total lack of birds or bees had made his situation seem like a crazy dream. Standing outside the cave, he watched the high dot shoot across the heavens and disappear to the south. A little later he went to bed.

Early in the morning eight helicopters went over, moving in line abreast. Spread out a hundred yards apart from each other, they floated fifty feet above the tree-tops. What they hoped to see beneath the concealing mass of vegetation was a mystery but it was obvious that they were searching all the same.

Going through the motions, thought Leeming as he watched them drift beyond his hiding-place. They had been ordered to look around, therefore they were looking around even though there was nothing to be seen. The pilots were enjoying a pleasant ride on the pretext that orders must be obeyed. In all probability the brasshat who had issued the command had never looked down into a forest in his life but, by virtue of his rank, was a self-styled authority upon the subject of how to find a flea in a dog's home. Baloney baffles brains in any part of the cosmos. Leeming had long nursed a private theory that wars do not end with victory for the side with the most brains: they are terminated by the defeat of the side with the most dopes. Also, that wars are prolonged because there is stiff competition in general imbecility.

By the end of the fourth day he was bored to tears. Squatting in a cave was not his idea of the full life and he could no longer resist the urge to get busy. He'd have to bestir himself before long in order to replenish his food supplies. The time had come, he felt, to make a start on the tedious chore of shifting the hidden dump southward and installing it in the cave.

Accordingly he set forth at dawn and pushed to the north as fast as he could go. This activity boosted his spirits considerably and he had to suppress the desire to whistle as he went along. In his haste he was making noise enough and there was no sense in further advertising his coming to any patrols that might be prowling through the woods.

As he neared the scene of his landing his pace slowed to the minimum. Here, if anywhere, caution was imperative since there was no knowing how many of the foe might still be lurking in the area. By the time he came within easy reach of his cache he was slinking from tree to tree, pausing frequently to look ahead and listen.

It was a great relief to find that the food-dump had not been disturbed. The supply was intact, exactly as he had left it. There was no sign that the enemy had been anywhere near it or, for the matter of that, was within fifty miles of it at the present moment. Emboldened by this, he decided to go to the edge of the forest and have another look at the crater. It would be interesting to learn whether the local lifeform had shown enough intelligence to take away the ship's shattered remnants with the idea of establishing its origin. The knowledge that they had done so would not help him one little bit—but he was curious and temporarily afflicted with a sense of false security.

As quietly and carefully as a cat stalking a bird, he sneaked the short distance to the forest's rim, gained it a couple of hundred yards from where he'd expected to view the crater. Walking farther along the edge of the trees, he stopped and stared at the graveyard of his ship, his attention concentrated upon it to the exclusion of all else. Many distorted hunks of metal still lay around and it was impossible to tell whether any of the junk had been removed.

Swinging his gaze to take in the total blast area, he was dumbfounded to discover three helicopters parked in line close to the trees. They were a quarter mile away, apparently unoccupied and with nobody hanging around. That meant their crews must be somewhere nearby. At once he started to back into the forest, his hairs tickling with alarm. He had taken only two steps when fallen leaves crunched behind him, something hard rammed into the middle of his back and a voice spoke in harsh, guttural tones.

"Smooge!" it said.

Bitterness at his own folly surged through Leeming's soul as he turned around to face the speaker. He found himself confronted by a humanoid six inches shorter than himself but almost twice as broad; a squat, powerful creature wearing dun-coloured uniform, a metal helmet and grasping a lethal instrument recognisable as some kind of gun. This character had a scaly, lizardlike skin, horn-covered eyes and no eyelids. He watched Leeming with the cold, unwinking stare of a rattlesnake.

"Smooge!" he repeated, giving a prod with the gun.

Raising his hands, Leeming offered a deceitful smile and said in fluent Cosmoglotta, "There is no need for this. I am a friend, an ally."

58

It was a waste of breath. Either the other did not understand Cosmoglotta or he could recognise a thundering lie when it was offered. His reptilian face showed not the slightest change of expression, his eyes retained their blank stare as he emitted a shrill whistle. Leeming noticed that his captor performed this feat without pursing his lips, the sound apparently coming straight from the throat.

Twenty more of the enemy responded by emerging from the forest at a point near where the helicopters were stationed. Their feet made distinct thuds as they ran with the stubby, clumping gait of very heavy men. Surrounding Leeming, they examined him with the same expressionless state that lacked surprise, curiosity or any other human trait. Next they gabbled together in a language slightly reminiscent of the crazy talk he had interrupted in space.

"Let me elucidate the goose."

"Dry up—the bostaniks all have six feet."

"I am a friend, an ally," informed Leeming, with suitable dignity.

This statement caused them to shut up with one accord. They gave him a mutual snake-look and then the biggest of them asked, "Snapnose?"

"I'm a Combine scout from far, far away," asserted Leeming, swearing it upon an invisible Bible. "As such I demand to be released."

It meant nothing whatever. Nobody smiled, nobody kissed him and it was obvious that none knew a word of Cosmoglotta. They were ill-educated types with not an officer among the lot.

"Now look here," he began, lowering his arms.

"Smooge!" shouted his captor, making a menacing gesture with the gun.

Leeming raised his arms again and glowered at them.

Now they held a brief conversation containing frequent mention of cheese and spark-plugs. It ended to their common satisfaction after which they searched him. This was done by the simple method of confiscation, taking everything in his possession including his braces.

That done, they chivvied him toward the helicopters. Perforce he went, trudging surlily along while holding up his pants with his hands. The pants were supposed to be self-supporting, the braces having been worn out of sheer pessimism, but he had lost a good deal of weight during his space trip, his middle was somewhat reduced in circumference and he had no desire to exhibit his posterior to alien eyes.

At command he climbed into a helicopter, turned quickly to slam the door in the hope that he might be able to lock them out long enough to take to the air without getting shot. They did not give him a chance. One was following close upon his heels and was halfway through the door even as he turned. Four more piled in. The pilot took his seat, started the motor. Overhead vanes jerked, rotated slowly, speeded up.

The 'copter bounced a couple of times, left the ground, soared into the purplish sky. It did not travel far. Crossing the wide expanse of moorland and the woods beyond, it descended upon the large village that Leeming had roared over only a few days ago. Gently it landed upon a concrete square at the back of a grim-looking building that, to Leeming's mind, resembled a military barracks or an asylum for the insane.

Here, they entered the building, hustled him along a corridor and into a stone-walled cell. They slammed and locked the heavy door in which was a small barred grille. A moment later one of them peered between the bars.

"We shall bend Murgatroyd's socks," announced the face reassuringly.

"Thanks," said Leeming. "Damned decent of you."

The face went away. Leeming walked ten times around the cell before sitting on a bare wooden plank that presumably was intended to serve as both seat and bed. There was no window through which to look upon the outside world, no opening other than the door. Resting his elbows on his knees, he held his face in his hands.

God, what a chump he'd been. If only he had remained content to take from the cache all the food he could carry and get away fast. If only he had accepted the good fortune of finding the food-dump intact and been satisfied to grab and run. But no, he had to be nosey and walk right into a trap. Perhaps the nervous strain of his long journey or something peculiar about the atmosphere of this planet had made him weak-minded. Whatever the reason, he was caught and ready for the chop.

As for his future prospects, he did not care to guess at them. It was known that the Combine had taken several hundreds of prisoners, mostly settlers on outpost worlds who'd been attacked without warning. Their fate was a mystery. Rumour insisted that the various lifeforms belonging to the Combine had widely different notions of how to handle the prisoner-of-war problem and that some were less humane than others. Since nothing whatever was known about the lifeform inhabiting this particular world the tactics they favoured were a matter for speculation or, in his own case, grim experience.

It was said—with what truth nobody knew—that the Lathians, for instance, treated as bona fide prisoners-of-war only those who happened to be captured unarmed and that anyone taken while bearing a weapon was slaughtered out of hand. Also that possession of a knife was regarded as justification for immediate murder providing that the said knife came within their definition of a weapon by having a blade longer than its owner's middle finger. This story might be ten miles wide of the facts. The space service always had been a happy hunting ground for incurable crap-mongers.

How long he sat there he did not know. They had deprived him of his watch, he could not observe the progress of the sun and had no means of estimating the time. But after a long while a guard opened the door, made an unmistakable gesture that he was to come out. He exited, found a second guard waiting in the corridor. With one in the lead and the other following, he was conducted through the building and into a large office.

The sole occupant was an autocratic specimen seated behind a desk on which was arrayed the contents of the prisoner's pockets. Leeming came to a halt before the desk, still holding up his pants. The guards positioned themselves either side of the door and managed to assume expressions of blank servility.

In fluent Cosmoglotta, the one behind the desk said, "I am Major Klavith. You will address me respectfully as becomes my rank. Do you understand?"

"Yes."

"What is your name, rank and number?"

"John Leeming, Lieutenant, 47926."

"Your species?"

"Terran. Haven't you ever seen a Terran before?"

"I am asking the questions," retorted Klavith, "and you will provide the answers." He paused to let that sink in, then continued. "You arrived here in a ship of Terran origin, did you not?"

"Sure did," agreed Leeming, with relish.

Bending forward, Klavith demanded with great emphasis, "On which planet was your vessel refuelled?"

There was silence as Leeming's thoughts moved fast. Obviously they could not credit that he had reached here non-stop because such a feat was far beyond their own technical ability. Therefore they believed that he had been assisted by some world within the Combine's ranks. He was being ordered to name the traitors. It was a wonderful opportunity to create dissension but unfortunately he was unable to make good use of it. He'd done no more than scout around hostile worlds, landing on none of them, and for the life of him he could not name or describe a Combine species anywhere on his route.

"Are you going to tell me you don't know?" prompted Klavith sarcastically.

"I do and I don't," Leeming responded. "The world was named to me only as XB173. I haven't the faintest notion of what you call it or what it calls itself."

"In the morning we shall produce comprehensive starmaps and you will mark thereon the exact location of this world. Between now and then you had better make sure that your memory will be accurate." Another long pause accompanied by the cold, lizardlike stare of his kind. "You have given us a lot of trouble. I have been flown here because I am the only person on this planet who speaks Cosmoglotta."

"The Lathians speak it."

"We are not Lathians as you well know. We are Zangastans. We do not slavishly imitate our allies in everything. The Combine is an association of free peoples."

"That may be your opinion. There are others."

"I am not in the least bit interested in other opinions. And I am not here to bandy words with you on the subject of interstellar politics." Surveying the stuff that littered his desk, Klavith poked forward the pepper-pot. "When you were caught you were carrying this container of incendiary powder. We know what it is because we have tested it. Why were you supplied with it?"

"It was part of my emergency kit."

"Why should you need incendiary powder in an emergency kit?"

"To start a fire to cook food or to warm myself," said Leeming, mentally damning the unknown inventor of emergency kits.

"I do not believe you. See where I am pointing: an automatic lighter. Is that not sufficient?"

"Those lighters wear out or become exhausted."

"Neither does the powder last for ever. You are lying to me. You brought this stuff for purposes of sabotage."

"Fat lot of good I'd do starting a few blazes umpteen millions of miles from home. When we hit the Combine we do it harder and more effectively."

"That may be so," Klavith conceded. "But I am far from satisfied with your explanation."

"If I gave you the true one you wouldn't believe it."

"Let me be the judge of that."

"All right. The powder was included in my kit merely because some high-ranking official thought it a wonderful idea."

"And why should he think so?" Klavith urged.

"Because any idea thought up by him must be wonderful."

"I don't see it."

"Neither do I. But *he* does and his opinion counts."

"Not with me it doesn't," Klavith denied. "Anyway, we intend to analyse this powder. Obviously it does not burst into flame when air reaches it, otherwise it would be too risky to carry. It must be in direct contact with an inflammable substance before it will function. A ship bearing a heavy load of this stuff could destroy a lot of crops. Enough systematic burning would starve an entire species into submission, would it not?"

Leeming did not answer.

"I suggest that one of your motives in coming here was to test the military effectiveness of this powder."

"What, when we could try it on our own wastelands without the bother of transporting it partway across a galaxy?"

"That is not the same as inflicting it upon an enemy."

"If I'd toted it all the way here just to do some wholesale burning," Leeming pointed out, "I'd have brought a hundred tons and not a couple of ounces."

Klavith could not find a satisfactory answer to that so he changed the subject by poking another object on his desk. "I have identified this thing as a midget camera. It is a remarkable instrument and cleverly made. But since aerial photography is far easier, quicker, wider in scope and more efficient than anything you could achieve with this gadget, I see no point in you being equipped with it."

"Neither do I," agreed Leeming.

"Then why did you continue to carry it?"

"Because it seemed a darned shame to throw it away."

This reason was accepted without dispute. Grabbing the camera, Klavith put it in his pocket.

"I can understand that. It is as beautiful as a jewel. Henceforth it is my personal property." He showed his teeth in what was supposed to be a triumphant grin. "The spoils of conquest." With contemptuous generosity he picked up the braces and tossed them at Leeming. "You may have these back. Put them on at once—a prisoner should be properly dressed while in my presence." He watched in silence as the other secured his pants, then said, "You were also in possession of a luminous compass. That I can understand. It is about the only item that makes sense."

Leeming offered no comment.

"Except perhaps for this." Klavith took up the stink-gun. "Either it is a mock weapon or it is real." He pulled the trigger a couple of times and nothing happened. "Which is it?"

"Real."

"Then how does it work?"

"To prime it you must press the barrel inward."

"That must be done every time you are about to use it?"

"Yes."

"In that case it is nothing better than a compressed-air gun?"

"Correct."

"I find it hard to credit that your authorities would arm you with anything so primitive," opined Klavith, showing concealed suspicion.

"Such a gun is not to be despised," offered Leeming. "It has its advantages. It needs no explosive ammunition. It will fire any missile that fits its barrel and it is comparatively silent. Moreover, it is just as intimidating as any other kind of gun."

"You argue very plausibly," Klavith admitted, "but I doubt whether you are telling me the whole truth."

"There's nothing to stop you trying it and seeing for yourself," Leeming invited. His stomach started jumping at the mere thought of it.

"I intend to do just that." Switching to his own language, Klavith let go a flood of words at one of the guards.

Showing some reluctance, the guard propped his rifle

against the wall, crossed the room and took the gun. Under Klavith's instructions, he put the muzzle to the floor and shoved. The barrel sank back, popped forward when the pressure was released. Pointing the gun at the wall he squeezed the trigger.

The weapon went *phut*! A tiny pellet burst on the wall and its contents immediately gasified. For a moment Klavith sat gazing in puzzlement at the damp spot. Then the awful stench hit him. His face took on a peculiar mottling, he leaned forward and spewed with such violence that he fell off his chair.

Holding his nose with his left hand, Leeming snatched the compass from the desk with his right and raced for the door. The guard who had fired the gun was now rolling on the carpet and trying to turn himself inside-out with such single-minded concentration that he neither knew nor cared what anyone else was doing. By the door the other guard had dropped his rifle while he leaned against the wall and emitted a rapid succession of violent whoops. Not one of the three was in any condition to pull up his own socks much less get in the way of an escapee.

Still gripping his nostrils, Leeming jerked open the door, dashed along the passage and out of the building. Hearing the clatter of his boots, three more guards rushed out of a room, pulled up as if held back by an invisible hand and threw their dinners over each other.

Outside, Leeming let go his nose. His straining lungs took in great gasps of fresh air as he sprinted toward the helicopter that had brought him here. This machine provided his only chance of freedom since the barracks and the entire village would be aroused at any moment and he could not hope to outrun the lot on foot.

Reaching the helicopter, he clambered into it, locked its

door. The alien controls did not baffle him because he had made careful note of them during his previous ride. Still breathing hard while his nerves twanged with excitement, he started the motor. The vanes began to turn.

Nobody had yet emerged from the stench-ridden exit he had used but somebody did come out of another door farther along the building. This character was unarmed and apparently unaware that anything extraordinary had taken place. But he did know that the humming helicopter was in wrong possession. He yelled and waved his arms as the vanes speeded up. Then he dived back into the building, came out holding a rifle.

The 'copter made its usual preliminary bumps, then soared. Below and a hundred yards away the rifle went off like a fire-cracker. Four holes appeared in the machine's plastic dome, something nicked the lobe of Leeming's left ear and drew blood, the tachometer flew to pieces on the instrument-board. A couple of fierce, hammerlike clunks sounded on the engine but it continued to run without falter and the 'copter gained height.

Bending sidewise, Leeming looked out and down through the perforated dome. His assailant was frantically shoving another magazine into the gun. A second burst of fire came when the 'copter was five hundred feet up and scooting fast. There came a sharp ping as a sliver of metal flew off the tail-fan but that was the only hit.

Leeming took another look below. The marksman had been joined by half a dozen others, all gazing skyward. None were attempting to shoot because the fugitive was now out of range. Even as he watched, the whole bunch of them ran into the building, still using the smell-free door. He could give a guess where they were heading for, namely, the radio-room.

The sight killed any elation he might have enjoyed. He had the sky to himself but it wasn't going to be forever. Now the moot question was whether he could keep it to himself long enough to make distance before he landed in the wilds and took to his heels again.

Chapter 5

Definitely he was not escaping the easy way. In many respects he was worse off than he'd been before. Afoot in the forest he'd been able to trudge around in concealment, feed himself, get some sleep. Now the whole world knew—or soon would know—that a Terran was on the loose. To keep watch while flying he needed eyes in the back of his head and even those wouldn't save him if something superfast such as a jetplane appeared. And if he succeeded in dumping his machine unseen he'd have to roam the world without a weapon of any kind.

Mentally he cursed the extreme haste with which he had dashed out of that room. The guard who'd fired the stinkgun had promptly collapsed upon it, hiding it with his body, but there might have been time to roll the fellow out of the way and snatch it up. And by the door had been two rifles either of which he could have grabbed and taken with him. He awarded himself the Idiot's Medal for passing up these opportunities despite the knowledge that at the time his only concern had been to hold his breath long enough to reach uncontaminated air.

Yes, his sole object had been to race clear of a paralysing nausea—but that needn't have stopped him from swiping a gun if he'd been quicker on the uptake. Perhaps there was a gun aboard the 'copter. Flying at two thousand feet, he was trying to keep full attention six ways at once, before, behind, to either side, above and below. He couldn't do that and examine the machine's interior as well. The search would have to wait until after he had landed.

By now he was some distance over the forest in which he'd been wandering. It struck him that when he'd been captured and taken away two helicopters had remained parked in this area. Possibly they had since departed for an unknown base. Or perhaps they were still there and about to rise in response to a radioed alarm.

His alertness increased, he kept throwing swift glances around in all directions while the machine hummed onward. After twenty minutes a tiny dot arose from the far horizon. At that distance it was impossible to tell whether it was a 'copter, a jetplane, or what. His motor chose this moment to splutter and squirt a thin stream of smoke. The whirling vanes hesitated, resumed their steady *whup-whup*.

Leeming sweated with anxiety and watched the faraway dot. Again the motor lost rhythm and spurted more smoke. The dot grew a little larger but was moving at an angle that showed it was not heading straight for him. Probably it was the herald of an aerial hunt that would find him in short time.

The motor now became asthmatic, the vanes slowed, the 'copter lost height. Greasy smoke shot from its casing in a series of forceful puffs, a fishy smell came with them. If a bullet had broken an oil-line, thought Leeming, he couldn't keep up much longer. It would be best to descend while he still retained some control.

As the machine lowered he swung its tail-fan in an effort to zig-zag and find a suitable clearing amid the mass of trees. Down he went to one thousand feet, to five hundred, and nowhere could he see a gap. There was nothing for it but to use a tree as a cushion and hope for the best.

Reversing the tail-fan to arrest his forward motion, he sank into an enormous tree that looked capable of supporting a house. Appearances proved deceptive for the huge branches were very brittle and easily gave way under the weight imposed upon them. To the accompaniment of repeated cracks the 'copter fell through the foliage in a rapid series of halts and jolts that made its occupant feel as though locked in a barrel that was bumping down a steep flight of stairs.

The last drop was the longest but ended in thick bushes and heavy undergrowth that served to absorb the shock. Leeming crawled out with bruised cheekbone and shaken frame. Blood slowly oozed from the ear-lobe that had been grazed by a bullet. He gazed upward. There was now a wide hole in the overhead vegetation but he doubted whether it would be noticed by any aerial observer unless flying very low.

The 'copter lay tilted to one side, its bent and twisted vanes forced to a sharp angle with the drive-shaft, bits of twig and bark still clinging to their edges. Hurriedly he searched the big six-seater cabin for anything that might prove useful. Of weapons there were none. In the tool-box he did find a twenty-inch spanner of metal resembling bronze and this he confiscated thinking it better than nothing.

Under the two seats at the rear he discovered neat compartments filled with alien food. It was peculiar stuff and not particularly appetising in appearance but right now he was hungry enough to gnaw a long-dead goat covered with flies. So he tried a circular sandwich made of what looked and tasted like two flat disks of unleavened bread with a thin layer of white grease between them. It went down, stayed down and made him feel better. For all he knew the grease might have been derived from a pregnant lizard. He was long past caring. His belly demanded more and he ate another two sandwiches.

There was quite a stack of these sandwiches plus a goodly number of blue-green cubes of what seemed to be some highly compressed vegetable. Also a can of sawdust that smelled like chopped peanuts and tasted like a weird mixture of minced beef and seaweed. And finally a plastic bottle filled with mysterious white tablets.

Taking no chances on the tablets, he slung them into the undergrowth but retained the bottle which would serve for carrying water. The can holding the dehydrated stuff was equally valuable; it was strong, well-made and would do duty as a cooking utensil. He now had food and a primitive weapon but lacked the means of transporting the lot. There was far too much to go into his pockets.

While he pondered this problem something howled across the sky about half a mile to the east. The sound had only just died away in the distance when something else whined on a parallel course half a mile to the west. Evidently the hunt was on.

Checking his impulse to run to some place better hidden from above, he took a saw-toothed instrument out of the tool-kit, used it to remove the canvas covering from a seat. This formed an excellent bag, clumsy in shape, without straps or handles, but of just the right size. Filling it with his supplies, he made a last inspection of the wrecked helicopter and noticed that its tiny altimeter-dial was fronted with a magnifying lens. The rim holding the lens was strong and stubborn, he had to work carefully to extract the lens without breaking it.

Under the engine-casing he found the reservoir of a windshield water-spray. It took the form of a light metal bottle holding about one quart. Detaching it, he emptied it, filled it with fuel from the 'copter's tank. These final acquisitions gave him the means of making a quick fire. Klavith could keep the automatic lighter and the pepper-pot and burn down the barracks with them. He, Leeming, had got something better. A lens does not exhaust itself or wear out. He was so gratified with his loot he forgot that a lens was somewhat useless night-times.

The unseen jetplanes screamed back, still a mile apart and on parallel courses. This showed that the hunt was being conducted systematically with more machines probing the air in other directions. Having failed to find the missing 'copter anywhere within the maximum distance it could travel since it was stolen, they'd soon realise that it had landed and start looking for it from lower altitude. That meant a painstaking survey from little more than tree-top height.

Now that he was all set to go he wasn't worried about how soon the searchers spotted the tree-gap and the 'copter. In the time it would take them to drop troops on the spot he could flee beyond sight or sound, becoming lost within the maze of trees. The only thing that bothered him was the possibility that they might have some species of trained animal capable of tracking him wherever he went.

He didn't relish the idea of a Zangastan land-octopus, or whatever it might be, snuffling up to him in the middle of the night and embracing him with rubbery tentacles while he was asleep. There were several people back home for whom such a fate would be more suitable, professional loud-shouters who'd be shut up for keeps. However, chances had to be taken. Shouldering his canvas bag he left the scene.

By nightfall he'd put about four miles between himself and the abandoned helicopter. He could not have done more even if he'd wished; the stars and three tiny moons did not provide enough light to permit further progress. Aerial activity continued without abate during the whole of this time but ceased when the sun went down.

The best sanctuary he could find for the night was a depression between huge tree-roots. With rocks and sods he built a screen at one end of it, making it sufficiently high to conceal a fire from anyone stalking him at ground level. That done, he gathered a good supply of dry twigs, wood chips and leaves. With everything ready he suddenly discovered himself lacking the means to start a blaze. The lens was useless in the dark; it was strictly for day-time only, beneath an unobscured sun.

This started him on a long spell of inspired cussing after which he hunted around until he found a stick with a sharply splintered point. This he rubbed hard and vigorously in the crack of a dead log. Powdered wood accumulated in the channel as he kept on rubbing with all his weight behind the stick. It took twenty-seven minutes of continuous effort before the wood-powder glowed and gave forth a thin wisp of smoke. Quickly he stuck a splinter wetted with 'copter fuel into the middle of the faint glow and at once it burst into flame. The sight made him feel as triumphant as if he'd won the war single-handed.

Now he got the fire going properly. The crackle and spit of it was a great comfort in his loneliness. Emptying the beef-seaweed compound onto a glossy leaf half the size of a blanket, he three-quarters filled the can with water, stood it on the fire. To the water he added a small quantity of the stuff on the leaf, also a vegetable cube and hoped that the result would be a hot and nourishing soup. While waiting for this alien mixture to cook he gathered more fuel, stacked it nearby, sat close to the flames and ate a grease sandwich.

After the soup had simmered for some time he put it aside to cool sufficiently to be sipped straight from the can. When eventually he tried it the stuff tasted much better than expected, thick, heavy and now containing a faint flavour of mushrooms. He absorbed the lot, washed the can in an adjacent stream, dried it by the fire and carefully refilled it with the compound on the leaf. Choosing the biggest lumps of wood from his supply, he arranged them on the flames to last as long as possible, and lay down within warming distance.

It was his intention to spend an hour or two considering his present situation and working out his future plans. But the soothing heat and the satisfying sensation of a full paunch lulled him to sleep within five minutes. He sprawled in the jungle with the great tree towering overhead, its roots rising on either side, the fire glowing near his feet while he emitted gentle snores and enjoyed one of the longest, deepest sleeps he had ever known.

The snooze lasted ten hours so that when he awoke he was only partway through the lengthy night. His eyes opened to see stars glimmering through the tree-gaps and for a moody moment they seemed impossibly far away. Rested but cold, he sat up and looked beyond his feet. Nothing could be seen of the fire. It must have burned itself out. He wished most heartily that he had awakened a couple of times and added more wood. But he had slept solidly, almost as if drugged. Perhaps some portion of that alien fodder was a drug in its effect upon the Terran digestive system.

Edging toward where the fire had been he felt around it. The ground was warm. His exploring hand went farther, plunged into hot ash. Three or four sparks gleamed fitfully and he burned a finger. Grabbing a twig he dunked it in the fuel-bottle and then used it to stir the embers. It flamed like a torch. Soon he had the fire going again and the coldness crept away.

Chewing a sandwich, he let his mind toy with current problems. The first thought that struck him was that he'd missed another chance when looting the helicopter. He had taken one seat-cover to function as a bag; if he'd had the hoss-sense to rob all the other seats and cut their covers wide open he'd have provided himself with bedclothes. Night-times he was going to miss his blankets unless somehow he could keep a fire going continuously. The seat-covers would have served to keep him wrapped and warm.

Damning himself for his stupidity he played with the idea of returning to the 'copter and making good the deficiency. Then he decided that the risk was too great. He'd been caught once by his own insistence upon returning to the scene of the crime and he'd be a prize fool to let himself be trapped the same way again.

For the time being he'd have to cope as best he could without blankets or anything in lieu thereof. If he shivered it was nobody's fault but his own. A wise, far-seeing Providence had created the dull-witted especially to do all the suffering. It was right and proper that he should pay for his blunders with his fair quota of discomfort.

Of course, even the sharpest brain could find itself ensnared by sheer hard luck or by misfortunes impossible to foresee. Chance operates for and against the individual with complete haphazardness. All the same, the bigger the blow the greater the need to use one's wits in countering it. Obstacles were made to be surmounted and not to be wept over.

Employing his wits to the best of his ability, he came to several conclusions. Firstly, that it was not enough merely to remain free because he had no desire to spend the rest of his natural life hiding upon an alien world. Somehow he must get off the planet and metaphorically kiss it goodbye forever.

Secondly, that there was no way of leaving except by spaceship, no way of returning to Earth except by spaceship. Therefore he must concentrate upon the formidable task of stealing a suitable ship. Any ship would not do. Making off with a war vessel or a cargo-boat or a passenger liner was far beyond his ability since all needed a complete crew to handle them. It would have to be a one-man or two-man scout-boat, fully fuelled and ready for long-range fight. Such ships existed in large numbers. But finding one and getting away with it was something else again.

Thirdly, even if by a near-miracle he could seize a scout-boat and vanish into space he'd have solved one major problem only to be faced by another identically the same. The ship could not reach Rigel, much less Earth, without at least one overhaul and refuelling on the way. No Combine group could be expected to perform this service for him unless he had the incredible luck to drop upon a species not in their right minds. His only answer to this predicament would be to land upon a planet with hiding-places, abandon his worn-out vessel and steal another. If either of these two ships failed to come up to scratch he might have to make yet another landing and grab a third one.

It was a grim prospect. The odds were of the order of a

million to one against him. All the same, there had been times when the millionth chance came off and there should be times when it would do so again.

There was another alternative that he dismissed as not worthy of consideration, namely, to stay put in the hope that the war would end reasonably soon and he'd be permitted to go home in peace. But the termination of the conflict had no fixed date. For all he knew, it might end when he was old and grey-bearded or fifty years after he was dead. All wars are the same in that there are times when they seem to have settled down for everlasting and lack of strife becomes almost unthinkable.

His ponderings ceased abruptly when something let go a deep-bellied cough and four green eyes stared at him out of the dark. Leaping to the fire, he snatched a flaming branch and hurled it in that direction. It described a blazing arc and fell into a bush.

The eyes blinked out, blinked on, then disappeared. There came the scuffling, slithering sounds of a cumbersome creature backing away fast. Gradually the noise died out in the distance. Leeming found himself unable to decide whether it had been one animal or two, whether it walked or crawled, whether it was the Zangastan equivalent of a prowling tiger or no more than a curious cow. At any rate, it had gone.

Sitting by the tree-trunk, he kept the fire going and maintained a wary watch until the dawn.

With the sunrise he breakfasted on a can of soup and a sandwich. Stamping out the fire, he picked up his belongings and headed to the south. This direction would take him farther from the centre of the search and, to his inward regret, would also put mileage between him and the concealed dump of real Terran food. On the other hand, a southward trek would bring him nearer to the equatorial belt in which he had seen three spaceports during his circumnavigation. Where there are ports there are ships.

Dawn had not lasted an hour before a jetplane shot overhead. A little later four helicopters came, all going slow and skimming the trees. Leeming squatted under a bush until they had passed, resumed his journey and was nearly spotted by a buoyant fan following close behind the 'copters. He heard the whoosh of it in the nick of time, flung himself flat beside a rotting log and did his best to look like a shapeless patch of earth. The thing's downward air-blast sprayed across his back as it floated above him. Nearby trees rustled their branches, dead leaves fluttered to ground. It required all his self-control to remain perfectly motionless while a pair of expressionless, snakelike eyes stared down.

The fan drifted away, its pilot fooled. Leeming got to his feet, glanced at his compass and pressed on. Energetically he cussed all fans, those who made them and those who rode them. They were slow, had short range and carried only one man. But they were dangerously silent. If a fugitive became preoccupied with his own thoughts, ceasing to be on the alert, he could amble along unaware of the presence of such a machine until he felt the air-blast.

Judging by this early activity the search was being pursued in manner sufficient to show that some high-ranking brasshat had been infuriated by his escape. It would not be Klavith, he thought. A major did not stand high enough in the military caste system. Somebody bigger and more influential had swung into action. Such a character would make an example of the unfortunate Klavith and every guard in the barrack-block. While warily he trudged onward he couldn't help wondering what Klavith's fate had been; quite likely anything from being boiled in oil to demotion to private, fourth class. On an alien world one cannot define disciplinary measures in Terran terms.

But it was a safe bet that if he, John Leeming, were to be caught again they'd take lots better care of him—such as by binding him in mummy-wrappings or amputating his feet or something equally unpleasant. He'd had one chance of freedom and had grabbed it with both hands; they wouldn't give him another opportunity. Among any species the escaper is regarded as a determined troublemaker deserving of special treatment.

All that day he continued to plod southward. Half a dozen times he sought brief shelter while air machines of one sort or another scouted overhead. At dusk he was still within the forest and the aerial snooping ceased. The night was a repetition of the previous one with the same regrets over the loss of his blankets, the same difficulty in making a fire. Sitting by the soothing blaze, his insides filled and his legs enjoying a welcome rest, he felt vaguely surprised that the foe had not thought to maintain the search through the night. Although he had shielded his fire from ground-level observation it could easily be spotted by a night-flying plane; it was a complete giveaway that he could not hope to extinguish before it was seen from above.

The next day was uneventful. Aerial activity appeared to have ceased. At any rate, no machines came his way. Perhaps for some reason known only to themselves they were concentrating the search elsewhere. He made good progress without interruption or molestation and, when the sun stood highest, used the lens to create a smokeless fire and give himself another meal. Again he ate well, since the insipid but satisfying alien food was having no adverse effect upon his system. A check on how much he had left showed that there was sufficient for another five or six days.

In the mid-afternoon of the second day afterward he reached the southern limit of the forest and found himself facing a broad road. Beyond it stretched cultivated flatlands containing several sprawling buildings that he assumed to be farms. About four miles away there arose from the plain a cluster of stone-built structures around which ran a high wall. At that distance he could not determine whether the place was a fortress, a prison, a hospital, a lunatic asylum, a factory protected by a top security barrier, or something unthinkable that Zangastans preferred to screen from public gaze. Whatever it was, it had a menacing appearance. His intuition told him to keep his distance from it.

Retreating a couple of hundred yards into the forest, he found a heavily wooded hollow, sat on a log and readjusted his plans. Faced with an open plain that stretched as far as the eye could see, with habitations scattered around and with towns and villages probably just over the horizon, it was obvious that he could no longer make progress in broad daylight. On a planet populated by broad, squat, lizard-skinned people a lighter-built and pink-faced Terran would stand out as conspicuously as a giant panda at a bishops' convention. He'd be grabbed on sight, especially if the radio and video had broadcast his description with the information that he was wanted.

The Combine included about twenty species, half of whom the majority of Zangastans had never seen. But they had a rough idea of what their co-partners looked like and they'd know a fugitive Terran when they found him. His chance of kidding his captors that he was an unfamiliar ally was mighty small; even if he could talk a bunch of peasants into half-believing him they'd hold him pending a check by authority.

Up to this moment he'd been bored by the forest with

its long parade of trees, its primitiveness, its silence, its lack of visible life. Now he viewed it as a sanctuary about to withdraw its protection. Henceforth he'd have to march by night and sleep by day—providing that he could find suitable hiding places in which to lie up. It was a grim prospect.

But the issue was clear-cut. If he wanted to reach a spaceport and steal a scout-boat he must press forward no matter what the terrain and regardless of risks. Alternatively, he must play safe by remaining in the forest, perpetually foraging for food around its outskirts, living the life of a hermit until ready for burial.

The extended day had several hours yet to go; he decided to have a meal and get some sleep before the fall of darkness. Accordingly he started a small fire with the lens, made himself a can of hot soup and had two sandwiches. Then he curled himself up in a wad of huge leaves and closed his eyes. The sun gave a pleasant warmth, sleep seemed to come easy. He slipped into a quick doze. Half a dozen vehicles buzzed and rattled along the nearby road. Brought wide awake, he cussed them with fervour, shut his eyes and tried again. It wasn't long before more passing traffic disturbed him.

This continued until the stars came out and two of the five small moons shed an eerie light over the landscape. He stood in the shadow of a tree, overlooking the road and waited for the natives to go to bed—if they did go to bed rather than hang bat-like by their heels from the rafters.

A few small trucks went past during this time. They had orange-coloured headlights and emitted puffs of white smoke or vapour. They sounded somewhat like model locomotives. Leeming got the notion that each one was steam-powered, probably with a flash-boiler fired with wood. There was no way of checking on this.

Ordinarily he wouldn't have cared a hoot how Zangastan trucks operated. Right now it was a matter of some importance. The opportunity might come to steal a vehicle and thus help himself on his way to wherever he was going. But as a fully qualified space-pilot he had not the vaguest idea of how to drive a steam-engine. Indeed, if threatened with the death of a thousand cuts he'd have been compelled to admit that he could not ride a bike.

While mulling his educational handicaps it occurred to him that he'd be dim-witted to sneak furtively through the night hoping for a chance to swipe a car or truck. The man of initiative *makes* his chances and does not sit around praying for them to be placed in his lap.

Upbraiding himself, he sought around in the gloom until he found a nice, smooth, fist-sized rock. Then he waited for a victim to come along. The first vehicle to appear was travelling in the wrong direction, using the farther side of the road. Most of an hour crawled by before two more came together, also on the farther side, one close behind the other.

Across the road were no trees, bushes or other means of concealment; he'd no choice but to keep to his own side and wait in patience for his luck to turn. After what seemed an interminable period a pair of orange lamps gleamed in the distance, sped toward him. As the lights grew larger and more brilliant he tensed in readiness.

At exactly the right moment he sprang from beside the tree, hurled the rock and leaped back into darkness. In his haste and excitement, he missed. The rock shot within an inch of the windshield's rim and clattered on the road. Having had no more than a brief glimpse of a vague, gesticulating shadow, the driver continued blithely on, unaware that he'd escaped a taste of thuggery.

Making a few remarks more emphatic than cogent, Leeming recovered the rock and resumed his vigil. The next truck showed up the same time as another one coming in the opposite direction. He shifted to behind the tree-trunk. The two vehicles passed each other at a point almost level with his hiding-place. Scowling after their diminishing beams he took up position again.

Traffic had thinned with the lateness of the hour and it was a good while before more headlights came beaming in the dark and running on the road's near side. This time he reacted with greater care and took better aim. A swift jump, he heaved the rock, jumped back.

The result was the dull *whup* of a hole being bashed through transparent plastic. A gutteral voice shouted something about a turkey-leg, this being an oath in local dialect. The truck rolled another twenty yards, pulled up. A broad, squat figure scrambled out of the cab and ran toward the rear in evident belief that he'd hit something.

Leeming, who had anticipated this move, met him with raised spanner. The driver didn't even see him; he bolted round the truck's tail and the spanner whanged on his pate and he went down without a sound. For a horrid moment Leeming thought that he had killed the fellow. Not that one Zangastan mattered more or less in the general scheme of things. But he had his own peculiar status to consider. Even the Terrans showed scant mercy to prisoners who killed while escaping.

However, the victim emitted bubbling snorts like a hog in childbirth and had plenty of life left in him. Dragging him onto the verge and under a tree, Leeming searched him, found nothing worth taking. The wad of paper money was devoid of value to a Terran who'd have no opportunity to spend it.

Just then a long, low tanker rumbled into view. Taking a tight grip on the spanner, Leeming watched its approach and prepared to fight or run as circumstances dictated. It went straight past, showing no interest in the halted truck.

Climbing into the cab, he had a look around, found that the truck was not steam-powered as he had thought. The engine was still running but there was no fire-box or anything resembling one. The only clue to power-source was a strong scent like that of alcohol mixed with a highly aromatic oil.

Tentatively he pressed a button and the headlights went out. He pressed it again and they came on. The next button produced a shrill, catlike yowl out front. The third had no effect whatever: he assumed that it controlled the self-starter. After some fiddling around he found that the solitary pedal was the footbrake and that a lever on the steering-wheel caused the machine to move forward or backward at speed proportionate to the degree of its shift. There was no sign of an ignition-switch, gear-change lever, headlight dipper or parking brake. The whole layout was a curious mixture of the ultra-modern and the antiquated.

Satisfied that he could drive it, he advanced the lever. The truck rolled forward, accelerated to a moderate pace and kept going at that. He moved the lever farther and the speed increased. The forest slid past on his left, the flatlands on his right and the road was a yellow ribbon streaming under the bonnet. Man, this was the life! Relaxing in his seat and feeling pretty good, he broke into ribald song.

The road split. Without hesitation he chose the arm that tended southward. It took him through a straggling village in which very few lights were visible. Reaching the country beyond he got onto a road running in a dead straight line across the plain. Now all five moons were in the sky, the landscape looked ghostly and forbidding. Shoving the lever a few more degrees, he raced onward.

After an estimated eighty miles he by-passed a city, met desultory traffic on the road but continued in peace and unchallenged. Next he drove past a high stone wall surrounding a cluster of buildings resembling those seen earlier. Peering upward as he swept by, he tried to see whether there were any guards patrolling the wall-top but it was impossible to tell without stopping the truck and getting out. That he did not wish to do, preferring to travel as fast and as far as possible while the going was good.

He'd been driving non-stop at high speed for several hours when a fire-trail bloomed in the sky and moved like a tiny crimson feather across the stars. As he watched, the feather floated round in a deep curve, grew bigger and brighter as it descended. A ship was coming in. Slightly to his left and far over the horizon there must be a spaceport.

Maybe within easy reach of him there was a scout-boat fully fuelled and just begging to be taken up. He licked his lips at the thought of it.

With its engine still running smoothly the truck passed through the limb of another large forest. He made mental note of the place lest within a short time he should be compelled to abandon the vehicle and take to his heels once more. After recent experiences he found himself developing a strong affection for forests; on a hostile world they were the only places offering anonymity and liberty.

Gradually the road tended leftward, leading him nearer and nearer toward where the hidden spaceport was presumed to be. The truck rushed through four small villages in rapid succession, all dark, silent and in deep slumber. Again the road split and this time he found himself in a quandary. Which arm would take him to the place of ships?

Nearby stood a signpost but its alien script meant nothing to him. Stopping the truck, he got out and examined his choice of routes as best he could in the poor light. The right arm seemed to be the more heavily used to judge by the condition of its surface. Picking the right side, he drove ahead.

Time went on so long without evidence of a spaceport that he was commencing to think he'd made a mistake when a faint glow appeared low in the forward sky. It came from somewhere behind a rise in the terrain, strengthened as he neared. He tooled up the hill, came over the crest and saw in a shallow valley a big array of floodlights illuminating buildings, concrete emplacements, blast-pits and four snouty ships standing on their tail-fins.

Chapter 6

He should have felt overjoyed. Instead he became filled with a sense of wariness and foreboding. A complete getaway just couldn't be as easy as he'd planned: there had to be a snag somewhere.

Edging the truck onto the verge, he braked and switched off his lights. Then he surveyed the scene more carefully. From this distance the four vessels looked too big and fat to be scout-boats, too small and out-of-date to be warships. It was very likely that they were cargo-carriers, probably of the trampship type.

Assuming that they were in good condition and fully prepared for flight, it was not impossible for an experienced, determined pilot to take one up single-handed. And if it was fitted with an autopilot he could keep it going for days and weeks. Without such assistance he was liable to drop dead through sheer exhaustion long before he was due to arrive anywhere worth reaching. The same problem did not apply to a genuine scout-boat because a one-man ship *had* to be filled with robotic aids. He estimated that these small merchantmen normally carried a crew of at least twelve apiece, perhaps as many as twenty.

Furthermore, he had seen a vessel coming in to land—so at least one of these four had not yet been serviced and was unfit for flight. There was no way of telling which one was the latest arrival. But a ship in the hand is worth ten someplace else. To one of his profession the sight of waiting vessels was irresistible.

Reluctance to part company with the truck until the last moment, plus his natural audacity, made him decide that there was no point in trying to sneak across the well-lit spaceport and reach a ship on foot. He'd do better to take the enemy by surprise, boldly drive into the place, park alongside a vessel and scoot up its ladder before they had time to collect their wits.

Once inside a ship with the airlock closed he'd be comparatively safe. It would take them far longer to get him out than it would to take him to master the strange controls and make ready to boost. He'd have shut himself inside a metal fortress and the first blast of its propulsors would clear the area for a couple of hundred yards around. Their only means of thwarting him would be to bring up heavy artillery and hole or topple the ship. By the time they'd dragged big guns to the scene he should be crossing the orbit of the nearest moon.

He consoled himself with these thoughts as he chivvied the truck onto the road and let it surge forward, but all the time he knew deep within his mind that this was to be a crazy gamble. There was a good chance that he'd grab himself a cold-dead rocket short of fuel and incapable of taking off. In that event all the irate Zangastans need do was sit around until he'd surrendered or starved to death. That they'd be so slow to react as to give him time to swap ships was a possibility almost non-existent.

Thundering down the valley road, the truck took a wide bend, raced for the spaceport's main gates. These were partly closed, leaving a yard-wide gap in the middle. An armed sentry stood at one side, behind him a hut containing others of the guard.

As the truck shot into view and roared toward him the sentry gaped at it in dumb amazement, showed the typical reaction of one far from the area of combat. Instead of pointing his automatic weapon in readiness to challenge he jumped into the road and tugged frantically to open the gates. The half at which he was pulling swung wide just in time for the truck to bullet through with a few inches to spare on either side. Now the sentry resented the driver's failure to say "Good morning!" or "Drop dead!" or anything equally courteous. Brandishing his gun, he performed a clumsy war-dance and screamed vitriolic remarks.

Concentrating on his driving to the exclusion of all else, Leeming went full tilt around the spaceport's concrete perimeter toward where the ships were parked. A bunch of lizard-skinned characters strolling along his path scattered and ran for their lives. Farther on a long, low motorised trolley loaded with fuel cylinders slid out of a shed, stopped in the middle of the road. Its driver threw himself off his seat and tried to dig himself out of sight as the truck wildly swerved around him and threatened to overturn.

Picking the most distant ship as the one it would take the foe longest to reach, Leeming braked by its tail-fins, jumped out of the cab, looked up. No ladder. Sprinting around the base, he found the ladder on the other side, went up it like a frightened monkey.

It was like climbing the side of a factory chimney. Halfway up he paused for breath, looked around. Diminished by distance and depth, a hundred figures were racing toward him. So also were four trucks and a thing resembling an armoured car. He resumed his climb, going as fast as he could but using great care because he was now so high that one slip would be fatal.

Anxiety increased as he neared the airlock at top. A few more seconds and he'd be out of shooting range. But they'd know that, too, and were liable to start popping at him while yet there was time. As he tried to make more speed his belly quirked at the thought of a last-moment bullet ploughing through him. His hands grabbed half a dozen rungs in quick succession, reached the airlock rim at which point he rammed his head against an unexpected metal rod. Surprised, he raised his gaze, found himself looking into the muzzle of a gun not as big as a cannon.

"Shatsi!" ordered the owner of the gun, making a downward motion with it. "Amash!"

For a mad moment Leeming thought of holding on with one hand while he snatched his opponent's feet with the other. He raised himself in readiness to grab. Either the fellow was impatient or read his intention because he hammered Lemming's fingers with the gun-barrel.

"Amash! Shatsi—amash!"

Leeming went slowly and reluctantly down the ladder. Black despair grew blacker with every step he descended. To be caught at the start of a chase was one thing; to be grabbed near the end of it, within reach of success, was something else. Hell's bells, he'd almost got away with it and that's what made the situation so bitter.

Hereafter they'd fasten him up twice as tightly and keep a doubly close watch upon him. Even if in spite of these precautions he broke free a second time, his chance of total escape would be too small to be worth considering; with an armed guard aboard every ship he'd be sticking his head in the trap whenever he shoved it into an airlock. By the looks of it he was stuck with this stinking world until such time as a Terran task-force captured it or the war ended, either of which events might take place a couple of centuries hence.

Reaching the bottom, he stepped onto concrete and turned around expecting to be given a kick in the stomach or a bust on the nose. Instead he found himself faced by a muttering but blank-faced group containing an officer whose attitude suggested that he was more baffled than enraged. Favouring Leeming with an unwinking stare, the officer let go a stream of incomprehensible gabble that ended on a note of query. Leeming spread his hands and shrugged.

The officer tried again. Leeming responded with another shrug and did his best to look contrite. Accepting this lack of understanding as something that proved nothing one way or the other, the officer bawled at the crowd. Four armed guards emerged from the mob, hustled the prisoner into the armoured car, slammed and locked the door and took him away.

At the end of the ride they shoved him into the back room of a rock house with two guards as company, the other two outside the door. Sitting on a low, hard chair, he sighed, gazed blankly at the wall for two hours. The guards also squatted, watched him as expressionlessly as a pair of snakes and said not a word.

At the end of that time a trooper brought food and water. Leeming gulped it down in silence, studied the wall for another two hours. Meanwhile his thoughts milled around.

It seemed pretty obvious, he decided, that the local gang had not realised that they'd caught a Terran. All their reactions showed that they were far from certain what they'd got.

To a certain extent this was excusable. On the Allied side of the battle was a federation of thirteen lifeforms, four of them human and three more very humanlike. The Combine consisted of an uneasy, precarious union of at least twenty lifeforms, three of which also were rather humanlike. Pending getting the answers from higher authority, this particular bunch of quasi-reptilians couldn't tell enemy from ally.

All the same, they were taking no chances and he could imagine what was going on while they kept him sitting on his butt. The officer would grab the telephone—or whatever they used in lieu—and call the nearest garrison town. The highest ranker there would promptly transfer responsibility to military headquarters. There, Klavith's alarm would have been filed and forgotten and a ten-star panjandrum would pass the query to the main beamstation. An operator would transmit a message asking the three humanlike allies whether they had lost track of a scout in this region.

When back came a signal saying, "No!" the local gang would realise that a rare bird had been caught deep within the spatial empire. They wouldn't like it. Holding-troops far behind the lines share all the glory and none of the grief and they're happy to let things stay that way. A sudden intrusion of the enemy where he's no right to be is an event disturbing to the even tenor of life and not to be greeted with cries of martial joy. Besides, from their viewpoint where one can sneak in, an army can follow, and it is disconcerting to be taken in force from the rear.

Then when the news got around Klavith would arrive at full gallop to remind everyone that this was not the first time Leeming had been captured, but the second. What would they do to him eventually? He was far from sure because previously he hadn't given them time to settle down to the job. It was most unlikely that they'd shoot him out of hand. If sufficiently civilised they'd cross-examine him and then imprison him for the duration. If uncivilised they'd dig up Klavith or maybe an ally able to talk Terran and milk the prisoner of every item of information he possessed by methods ruthless and bloody.

Back toward the dawn of history when conflict had been confined to one planet there had existed a protective device known as the Geneva Convention. It had organised neutral inspection of prison camps, brought occasional letters from home, provided food parcels that had kept alive many a captive who otherwise might have died.

There was nothing like that today. A prisoner had only two forms of protection, those being his own resources and the power of his side to retaliate against the prisoners they'd got. And the latter was a threat more potential than real. There cannot be retaliation without actual knowledge of maltreatment.

The day dragged on. The guards were changed twice. More food and water came. Eventually the one window showed that darkness was approaching. Eyeing the window furtively, Leeming decided that it would be suicidal to take a running jump at it under two guns. It was small and high, difficult to scramble through in a hurry. How he wished he had his own stink-gun now!

A prisoner's first duty is to escape. That means biding one's time with appalling patience until occurs an opportunity that may be seized and exploited to the utmost. He'd done it once and he must do it again. If no way of total escape existed he'd have to invent one.

The prospect before him was tough indeed; before long it was likely to become a good deal tougher. If only he'd been able to talk the local language, or any Combine language, he might have been able to convince even the linguistic Klavith that black was white. Sheer impudence can pay dividends. Maybe he could have landed his ship, persuaded them with smooth words, unlimited self-assurance and just the right touch of arrogance to repair and reline his propulsors and cheer him on his way never suspecting that they had been talked into providing aid and comfort for the enemy.

It was a beautiful dream but an idle one. Lack of ability to communicate in any Combine tongue had balled up such a scheme at the start. You can't chivvy a sucker into donating his pants merely by making noises at him. Some other chance must now be watched for and grabbed, swiftly and with both hands—providing that they were fools enough to permit a chance.

Weighing up his guards in the same way as he had estimated the officer, his earlier captors and Klavith, he didn't think that this species was numbered among the Combine's brightest brains. All the same they were broad in the back, sour in the puss and plenty good enough to put someone in the pokey and keep him there for a long, long time.

In fact they were naturals as prison wardens.

He remained in the house four days, eating and drinking at regular intervals, sleeping halfway through the lengthy nights, cogitating for hours and often glowering at his impassive guards. Mentally he concocted, examined and rejected a thousand ways of regaining his liberty, most of them spectacular, fantastic and impossible.

At one time he went so far as to try to stare the guards

into a hypnotic trance, gazing intently at them until his own eyeballs felt locked for keeps. It did not bother them in the least. They had the reptilian ability to remain motionless and outstare him until kingdom come.

Mid-morning of the fourth day the officer strutted in, yelled, "Amash! Amash!" and gestured toward the door. His tone and manner were decidedly unfriendly. Evidently someone had identified the prisoner as an Allied spacelouse.

Getting off his seat, Leeming walked out, two guards ahead, two behind, the officer in the rear. A box-bodied car sheathed in steel waited on the road. They urged him into it, locked it. A pair of guards stood on the rear platform hard against the doors and clung to the handrails. A third joined the driver at the front. The journey took thirteen hours, the whole of which the inmate spent jouncing around in complete darkness.

By the time the car halted Leeming had invented one new and exceedingly repulsive word. He used it immediately the rear doors opened.

"Quilpole—enk?" he growled. *"Enk?"*

"Amash!" bawled the guard, unappreciative of alien contributions to the vocabulary of invective. He gave the other a powerful shove.

With poor grace Leeming amashed. He glimpsed great walls rearing against the night and a zone of brilliant light high up before he was pushed through a metal portal and into a large room. Here a reception committee of six thuglike samples awaited him. One of the six signed a paper presented by the escort. The guards withdrew, the door closed, the six eyed the arrival with complete lack of amiability.

One of them said something in an authoritative voice and made motions indicative of undressing.

97

Leeming called him a smelly quilpole conceived in an alien marsh.

It did him no good. The six grabbed him, stripped him naked, searched every vestige of his clothing, paying special attention to seams and linings. They displayed the expert technique of ones who'd done this job countless times already, knew exactly where to look and what to look for. None showed the slightest interest in his alien physique despite that he was posing fully revealed in the raw.

Everything he possessed was put on one side and his clothes shied back at him. He dressed himself while they pawed through the loot and gabbled together. Satisfied that the captive now owned nothing more than was necessary to hide his shame, they led him through the farther door, up a flight of thick stone stairs, along a stone corridor and into a cell. The door slammed with a sound like that of the crack of doom.

In the dark of night eight small stars and one tiny moon shone through a heavily barred opening high up in one wall. Along the bottom of the gap shone a faint yellow glow from some outside illumination.

Fumbling around in the gloom he found a wooden bench against one wall. It moved when he lugged it. Dragging it beneath the opening he stood upon it but found himself a couple of feet too low to get a view outside. Though heavy, he struggled with it until he had it propped at an angle against the wall, then he crawled carefully up it and had a look between the bars.

Forty feet below lay a bare stone-floored space fifty yards wide and extending to the limited distance he could see rightward and leftward. Beyond the space a smooth-surfaced stone wall rising to his own level. The top of the wall angled at about sixty degrees to form a sharp apex ten inches above which ran a single line of taut wire, without barbs.

From unseeable sources to right and left poured powerful beams of light that flooded the entire area between cell-block and outer wall as well as a similarly wide space beyond the wall. There was no sign of life. There was only the wall, the flares of light, the overhanging night and the distant stars.

"So I'm in the jug," he said. "That's torn it!"

He jumped to the invisible floor and the slight thrust made the bench fall with a resounding crash. It sounded as if he had produced a rocket and let himself be whisked through the roof. Feet raced along the outside passage, light poured through a suddenly opened spyhole in the heavy metal door. An eye appeared in the hole.

"Sach invigia, faplap!" shouted the guard.

Leeming called him a flatfooted, duck-assed quilpole and added six more words, older, time-worn but still potent. The spyhole slammed shut. He lay on the hard bench and tried to sleep.

An hour later he kicked hell out of the door and when the spyhole opened he said, "Faplap yourself!"

After that he did sleep.

Breakfast consisted of one lukewarm bowl of stewed grain resembling millet and a mug of water. Both were served with disdain and eaten with disgust. It wasn't as good as the alien muck on which he had lived in the forest. But of course he hadn't been on convict's rations then; he'd been eating the meals of some unlucky helicopter crew.

Sometime later a thin-lipped specimen arrived in company with two guards. With a long series of complicated gestures this character explained that the prisoner was to learn a civilised language and, what was more, would learn it fast—by order. Education would commence forthwith.

Puzzled by the necessity, Leeming asked, "What about Major Klavith?"

"Snapnose?"

"Why can't Klavith do the talking? Has he been struck dumb or something?"

A light dawned upon the other. Making stabbing motions with his forefinger, he said, "Klavith—fat, fat, fat!"

"Huh?"

"Klavith—fat, fat, fat!" He tapped his chest several times, pretended to crumple to the floor, and succeeded in conveying that Klavith had expired with official assistance.

"Holy cow!" said Leeming.

In businesslike manner the tutor produced a stack of juvenile picture books and started the imparting process while the guards lounged against the wall and looked bored. Leeming co-operated as one does with the enemy, namely, by misunderstanding everything, mispronouncing everything and overlooking nothing that would prove him a linguistic moron.

The lesson ended at noon and was celebrated by the arrival of another bowl of gruel containing a hunk of stringy, rubbery substance resembling the hind end of a rat. He drank the gruel, sucked the portion of animal, shoved the bowl aside.

Then he pondered the significance of their decision to teach him how to talk. In bumping off the unfortunate Klavith they had become the victims of their own ruthlessness. They'd deprived themselves of the world's only speaker of Cosmoglotta. Probably they had a few others who could speak it stationed on allied worlds, but it would take time and trouble to bring one of those back here. Someone had blundered by ordering Klavith's execution; he was going to cover up the mistake by teaching the prisoner to squeal.

Evidently they'd got nothing resembling Earth's electronic brain-pryers and could extract information only by question-and-answer methods aided by unknown forms of persuasion. They wanted to know things and intended to learn them if possible. The slower he was to gain fluency the longer it would be before they put him on the rack, if that was their intention.

His speculations ended when the guards opened the door and ordered him out. Leading him along the corridor, down the stairs, they released him into a great yard filled with figures mooching aimlessly around under a bright sun. He halted in surprise.

Rigellians! About two thousand of them. These were allies, fighting friends of Terra. He looked them over with mounting excitement, seeking a few more familiar shapes amid the mob. Perhaps an Earthman or two. Or even a few humanlike Centaurians.

But there were none. Only rubber-limbed, pop-eyed Rigellians shuffling around in the dreary manner of those confronted with many wasted years and no perceivable future.

Even as he gazed at them he sensed something peculiar. They could see him as clearly as he could see them and, being the only Earthman, he was a legitimate object of attention, a friend from another star. They should have been crowding up to him, full of talk, seeking the latest news of the war, asking questions and offering information.

It wasn't like that at all. They took no notice of him, behaved as if the arrival of a Terran were of no consequence whatever. Slowly and deliberately he walked across the yard, inviting some sort of fraternal reaction. They got out of his way. A few eyed him furtively, the majority pretended to be unaware of his existence. Nobody offered a word of comfort. Obviously they were giving him the conspicuous brush-off.

He trapped a small group of them in a corner of the yard and demanded with ill-concealed irritation, "Any of you speak Terran?"

They looked at the sky, the wall, the ground, or at each other, and remained silent.

"Anyone know Centaurian?"

No answer.

"Well, how about Cosmoglotta?"

No reply.

Riled, he walked away and tried another bunch. No luck. Within an hour he had fired questions at two or three hundred without getting a single response. It puzzled him completely. Their manner was not contemptuous or hostile but something else. He tried to analyse it, came to the conclusion that for an unknown reason they were wary, they were afraid to speak to him.

Sitting on a stone step he watched them until a shrill whistle signalled that exercise-time was over. The Rigellians formed up in long lines in readiness to march back to their quarters. Leeming's guards gave him a kick in the pants and chivvied him to his cell.

Temporarily he dismissed the problem of unsociable allies. After dark was the time for thinking because then there was nothing else to do. He wanted to spend the remaining hours of daylight in studying the picture-books and getting well ahead with the local lingo while appearing to lay far behind. Fluency might prove an advantage some day. Too bad that he had never learned Rigellian, for instance.

So he applied himself fully to the task until print and pictures ceased to be visible. He ate his evening portion of mush, after which he lay on the bench, closed his eyes, set his mind to work.

In all of his hectic life he'd met no more than about twenty Rigellians. Never once had he visited their three closely bunched solar systems. What little he knew of them was hearsay evidence. It was said that their standard of intelligence was good, they were technologically efficient, they had been consistently friendly toward men of Earth since first contact nearly a thousand years ago. Fifty per cent of them spoke Cosmoglotta, about one per cent knew the Terran tongue.

Therefore if the average held up, several hundreds of those met in the yard should have been able to converse with him in one language or another. Why had they steered clear of him and maintained silence? And why had they been mighty unanimous about it?

Determined to solve this puzzle he invented, examined and discarded a dozen theories, all with sufficient flaws to strain the credulity. It was about two hours before he hit upon the obvious solution.

These Rigellians were prisoners deprived of liberty for an unknown number of years to come. Some of them must have seen an Earthman at one time or another. But all of them knew that in the Combine's ranks were a few species superficially humanlike. They couldn't swear to it that a Terran really was a Terran and they were taking no chances on him being a spy, an ear of the enemy planted among them to listen for plots.

That in turn meant something else: when a big mob of prisoners become excessively suspicious of a possible traitor in their midst it's because they have something to hide. Yes, that was it! He slapped his knee in delight. The Rigellians had an escape scheme in process of hatching and meanwhile were taking no chances.

They had been here plenty long enough to become at least bored, at most desperate, and seek the means to make a break. Having found a way out, or being in process of making one, they were refusing the take the risk of letting the plot be messed up by a stranger of doubtful origin. Now his problem was that of how to overcome their suspicions, gain their confidence and get himself included in whatever was afoot. To this he gave considerable thought.

Next day, at the end of exercise-time, a guard swung a heavy leg and administered the usual kick. Leeming promptly hauled off and punched him clean on the snout. Four guards jumped in and gave the culprit a thorough going over. They did it good and proper, with zest and effectiveness that no onlooking Rigellian could possibly mistake for a piece of dramatic play-acting. It was an object lesson and intended as such. The limp body was taken out of the yard and lugged upstairs, its face a mess of blood.

Chapter 7

It was a week before Leeming was fit enough to reappear in the yard. The price of confidence had proved rough, tough and heavy and his features were still an ugly sight. He strolled through the crowd, ignored as before, chose a soft spot in the sun and sat.

Soon afterward a prisoner sprawled tiredly on the ground a couple of yards away, watched distant guards and spoke in little more than a whisper.

"Where d'you come from?"

"Terra."

"How'd you get here?"

Leeming told him briefly.

"How's the war going?"

"We're pushing them back slowly but surely. But it'll take a long time to finish the job."

"How long do you suppose?"

"I don't know. It's anyone's guess." Leeming eyed him curiously. "What brought your bunch here?"

"We're not combatants but civilian colonists. Our government placed advance parties, all male, on four new planets that were ours by right of discovery. Twelve thousand of us altogether." The Rigellian paused while he looked carefully around, noted the positions of various guards. "The Combine descended on us in force. That was two years ago. It was easy. We weren't prepared for trouble, weren't adequately armed, didn't even know that a war was on."

"They grabbed your four planets?"

"You bet they did. And laughed in our faces."

Leeming nodded understanding. Cynical and ruthless claim-jumping had been the original cause of the fracas now extended across a great slice of the galaxy. On one planet a colony had put up an heroic resistance and died to the last man. The sacrifice had fired a blaze of fury, the Allies had struck back and were still striking good and hard.

"Twelve thousand, you said. Where are the others?"

"Scattered around in prisons like this one. You certainly picked a choice dump on which to sit out the war. The Combine has made this its chief penal planet. It's far from the fighting front, unlikely ever to be discovered. The local lifeform isn't much good for space-battles but plenty good enough to hold what its allies have captured. They're throwing up big jails all over the world. If the war goes on long enough this cosmic dump will become solid with prisoners."

"So your crowd has been here about two years?"

"Sure have—and it seems more like ten."

"And done nothing about it?"

"Nothing much," agreed the Rigellian. "Just enough to get forty of us shot for trying."

"Sorry," said Leeming sincerely.

"Don't let it bother you. I know exactly how you feel. The first few weeks are the worst. The idea of being pinned down for keeps can drive you crazy unless you learn to be philosophical about it." He mused awhile, indicated a heavily built guard patrolling by the farther wall. "A few days ago that lying swine boasted that already there are two hundred thousand Allied prisoners on this planet and added that by this time next year there would be two million. I hope he never lives to see it."

"I'm getting out of here," said Leeming.

"How?"

"I don't know yet. But I'm getting out. I'm not going to stay here and rot." He waited in the hope of some comment about others feeling the same way, perhaps evasive mention of a coming break, a hint that he might be invited to join in.

Standing up, the Rigellian murmured, "Well, I wish you luck. You'll need all you can get."

He ambled away, having betrayed nothing. A whistle blew, the guards shouted, "Merse, faplaps! Amash!" And that was that.

Over the next four weeks he had frequent conversations with the same Rigellian and about twenty others, picking up odd items of information but finding them peculiarly evasive whenever the subject of freedom came up. They were friendly, in fact cordial, but remained determindedly tightmouthed.

One day he was having a surreptitious chat and asked, "Why does everyone insist on talking to me secretively and in whispers? The guards don't seem to care how much you gab to one another."

"You haven't yet been cross-examined. If in the meantime they notice that we've had plenty to say to you they will try to force out of you everything we've said—with particular reference to ideas on escape."

Leeming immediately pounced upon the lovely word. "Ah, escape, that's all there is to live for right now. If anyone is thinking of making a bid maybe I can help them and they can help me. I'm a competent space-pilot and that fact is worth something."

The other cooled at once. "Nothing doing."

"Why not?"

"We've been behind walls a long time and have been taught many things that you've yet to learn."

"Such as?"

"We've discovered at bitter cost that escape attempts fail when too many know what is going on. Some planted spy betrays us. Or some selfish fool messes things up by pushing in at the wrong moment."

"I am neither a spy nor a fool. I'm certainly not enough of an imbecile to spoil my own chance of breaking free."

"That may be," the Regillian conceded. "But imprisonment creates its own special conventions. One firm rule we have established here is that an escape-plot is the exclusive property of those who concocted it and only they can make the attempt by that method. Nobody else is told about it. Nobody else knows until the resulting hullabaloo starts going. Secrecy is a protective screen that would-be escapers must maintain at all costs. They'll give nobody a momentary peek through it, not even a Terran and not even a qualified space-pilot."

"So I'm strictly on my own?"

"Afraid so. You're on your own in any case. We sleep in dormitories, fifty to a room. You're in a cell all by yourself. You're in no position to help with anything."

"I can damned well help myself," Leeming retorted angrily.

And it was his turn to walk away.

He'd been in the pokey just thirteen weeks when the tutor handed him a metaphorical firecracker. Finishing a session distinguished only by Leeming's dopiness and slowness to learn, the tutor scowled at him and gave forth to some point.

"You are pleased to wear the cloak of idiocy. But am I an idiot too? I do not think so! I am not deceived—you are far more fluent that you pretend. In seven days time I shall report to the Commandant that you are ready for examination."

"How's that again," asked Leeming, putting on a baffled frown.

"You will be questioned by the Commandant seven days hence."

"I have already been questioned by Major Klavith."

"That was verbal, Klavith is dead and we have no record of what you told him."

Slam went the door. Came the gruel and a jaundiced lump of something unchewable. The local catering department seemed to be obsessed by the edibility of a rat's buttocks. Exercise-time followed.

"I've been told they're going to put me through the mill a week from now."

"Don't let that scare you," advised the Rigellian. "They would as soon kill you as spit in the sink. But one thing keeps them in check."

"What's that?"

"The Allies are holding a stack of prisoners, too."

"Yes, but what they don't know they can't grieve over."

"There'll be more grief for the entire Zangastan species

if the victor finds himself expected to exchange very live prisoners for very dead corpses."

"You've made a point there," agreed Leeming. "Maybe it would help if I had nine feet of rope to dangle suggestively in front of the Commandant."

"It would help if I had a very large bottle of *vitx* and a shapely female to stroke my hair," sighed the Rigellian.

"If you can feel that way after two years of semi-starvation, what are you like on a full diet?"

"It's all in the mind," the Rigellian said. "I like to think of what might have been."

The whistle again. More intensive study while daylight lasted. Another bowl of ersatz porridge. Darkness and a few small stars peeping through the barred slot high up. Time seemed to stand still, as it does with a high wall around it.

He lay on the bench and produced thoughts like bubbles from a fountain. No place, positively no place is absolutely impregnable. Given brawn and brains, time and patience, there's always a way in or out. Escapees shot down as they bolted had chosen the wrong time and wrong place, or the right time but the wrong place, or the right place but the wrong time. Or they had neglected brawn in favour of brains, a common fault of the overcautious. Or they'd neglected brains in favour of brawn, a fault of the reckless.

With eyes closed he carefully reviewed the situation. He was in a cell with rock walls of granite hardness at least four feet thick. The only openings were a narrow gap blocked by five massive steel bars, also an armour-plated door in constant view of patrolling guards.

On his person he had no hacksaw, no lock-pick, no implement of any sort, nothing but the bedraggled clothes in which he reposed. If he pulled the bench to pieces and somehow succeeded in doing it unheard he'd acquire several large lumps of wood, a dozen six-inch nails and a couple of steel bolts. None of that junk would serve to open the door or cut the window-bars. And there was no other material available.

Outside stretched a brilliantly illuminated gap fifty yards wide that must be crossed to gain freedom. Then a smooth stone wall forty feet high, devoid of handholds. Atop the wall an apex much too sharp to give grip to the feet while stepping over an alarm-wire that would set the sirens going if either touched or cut.

The great wall completely encircled the entire prison. It was octagonal in shape and topped at each angle by a watch-tower containing guards, floodlights and guns. To get out, the wall would have to be surmounted right under the nose of itchy-fingered watchers, in bright light, without touching the wire. That wouldn't be the end of it either; beyond the wall was another illuminated area also to be crossed. An unlucky last-lapper could get over the wall by some kind of miracle, only to be shot to bloody shreds during his subsequent dash for darkness.

Yes, the whole set-up had the professional touch of those who knew what to do to keep prisoners in prison. Escape over the wall was well-nigh impossible though not completely so. If somebody got out of his cell or dormitory armed with a rope and grapnel, and if he had a daring confederate who'd break into the power-room and switch off everything at exactly the right moment, he might make it. Up the wall and over the dead, unresponsive alarm-wire in total darkness.

In a solitary cell there is no rope, no grapnel, nothing capable of being adapted as either. There is no desperate and trustworthy confederate. Even if these things had been available he'd have considered such a project as near-suicidal.

If he pondered once the most remote possibilities and took stock of the minimum resources needed, he pondered them a hundred times. By long after midnight he'd been beating his brains sufficiently hard to make them come up with anything, including ideas that were slightly mad.

For example: he could pull a plastic button from his jacket, swallow it and hope that the result would get him a transfer to hospital. True, the hospital was within the prison's confines but it might offer better opportunity to escape. Then he thought a second time, decided that an intestinal blockage would not guarantee his removal elsewhere. They might do no more than force a powerful purgative down his neck and thus add to his present discomforts.

As dawn broke he arrived at a final conclusion. Thirty, forty or fifty Rigellians working in a patient, determined group might tunnel under the wall and both illuminated areas and get away. But he had one resource and one only. That was guile. There was nothing else he could employ.

He let go a loud groan and complained to himself, "So I'll have to use both my heads!"

This inane remark percolated through the innermost recesses of his mind and began to ferment like yeast. After a while he sat up startled, gazed at what little he could see of the brightening sky and said in a tone approaching a yelp, "Yes, sure, that's it—*both* heads!"

Stewing the idea over and over again, Leeming decided by exercise-time that it was essential to have a gadget. A crucifix or a crystal ball provides psychological advantages too good to miss. His gadget could be of any shape, size or design, made of any material so long as it was visibly and undeniably a contraption. Moreover, its potency would be greater if not made from items obtainable within his cell such as parts of his clothing or pieces of the bench. Preferably it should be constructed of stuff from somewhere else and should convey the irresistible suggestion of a strange, unknown technology.

He doubted whether the Rigellians could help. Twelve hours per day they slaved in the prison's workshops, a fate that he would share after he'd been questioned and his aptitudes defined. The Rigellians made military pants and jackets, harness and boots, a small range of light engineering and electrical components. They detested producing for the enemy but their choice was a simple one: work or starve.

According to what he'd been told they hadn't the remotest chance of smuggling out of the workshops anything really useful such as a knife, chisel, hammer or hacksaw blade. At the end of each work period the slaves were paraded and none allowed to break ranks until every machine had been checked, every loose tool accounted for and locked away.

The first fifteen minutes of the mid-day break he spent searching the yard for any loose item that might somehow be turned to advantage. He wandered around with his gaze fixed on the ground like a worried kid seeking a lost coin. The only things he found were a couple of pieces of wood four inches square by one inch thick, and these he slipped into his pocket without having the vaguest notion of what he intended to do with them.

Finishing the hunt, he squatted by the wall, had a whispered chat with a couple of Rigellians. His mind wasn't on the conversation and the pair mooched off when a curious guard came near. Later another Rigellian edged up to him.

"Earthman, are you still going to get out of here?"

"You bet I am."

The other chuckled and scratched an ear, an action that his species used to express polite scepticism. "I think we've a better chance than you're ever likely to get."

Leeming shot him a sharp glance. "Why?"

"There are more of us and we're together," evaded the Rigellian, as though realising that he'd been on the point of saying too much. "What can one do on one's own?"

"Bust out and run like blazes first chance," said Leeming.

Just then he noticed the ring on the other's ear-scratching finger and became fascinated with it. He'd seen the modest ornament before. A number of Rigellians were wearing similar objects. So were some of the guards. These rings were neat affairs consisting of four or five turns of thin wire with the ends shaped and soldered to form the owner's initials.

"Where'd you dig up the jewellery?" he asked.

"Where did I get what?"

"The ring."

"Oh, that." Lowering his hand, the Rigellian studied the ring with satisfaction. "We make them ourselves in the workshops. It breaks the monotony."

"Mean to say the guards don't stop you?"

"They don't interfere. There's no harm in it. Besides, we've made quite a few for the guards themselves. We've made them some automatic lighters as well and could have turned out a lot for ourselves if we'd had any use for them." He paused, looked thoughtful and added, "We think the guards have been selling rings and lighters outside. At least, we hope so."

"Why?"

"Maybe they'll build up a nice, steady trade. Then when they are comfortably settled in it we'll cut supplies and demand a rake-off in the form of extra rations and a few unofficial privileges."

"That's a smart idea," approved Leeming. "It would help all concerned to have a high-pressure salesman pushing the goods in the big towns. How about putting me down for that job?"

Giving a faint smile, the Rigellian continued, "Handmade junk doesn't matter. But let the guards find that one small screwdriver is missing and there's hell to pay. Everyone is stripped naked on the spot and the culprit suffers."

"They wouldn't care about losing a small coil of that wire, would they?"

"I doubt it. There's plenty of it, they don't bother to check the stock. What can anyone do with a piece of wire?"

"Heaven alone knows," Leeming admitted. "But I want some all the same."

"You'll never pick a lock with it in a million moons," warned the other. "It's too soft and thin."

"I want enough to make a set of Zulu bangles. I sort of fancy myself in Zulu bangles."

"And what are those?"

"Never mind. Get me some of that wire—that's all I ask."

"You can steal it yourself in the near future. After you've been questioned they'll send you to the workshops."

"I want it before then. I want it just as soon as I can get it. The more the better and the sooner the better."

Going silent, the Rigellian thought it over, finally said, "If you've a plan in your mind keep it to yourself. Don't let slip a hint of it to anyone. Open your mouth once too often and somebody will beat you to it."

"Thanks for the good advice, friend," said Leeming. "Now how about a supply of wire?"

"See you this time tomorrow."

With that, the Rigellian left him, wandered into the crowd.

At the appointed hour the other was there, passed him the loot. "Nobody gave this to you, see? You found it lying in the yard. Or you found it hidden in your cell. Or you conjured it out of thin air. But nobody gave it to you."

"Don't worry. I won't involve you in any way. And thanks a million."

The wire was a thick, pocket-sized coil of tinned copper. When unrolled in the darkness of his cell it measured a little more than his own length, or about seven feet.

Leeming doubled it, waggled it to and fro until it broke, hid one half under the bottom of the bench. Then he spent a couple of hours worrying a nail out of the bench's end. It was hard going and it played hob with his fingers, but he persisted until the nail was free.

Finding one of the small squares of wood, he approximated its centre, stamped the nail-point into it with the heel of his boot. Footsteps sounded along the corridor, he shoved the stuff out of sight beneath the bench, lay down just in time before the spyhole opened. The light flashed on, a cold, Reptilian eye looked in, somebody grunted. The light cut off, the spyhole shut.

Resuming his task, Leeming twisted the nail one way and then the other, stamping on it with his boot from time to time. The task was tedious but at least it gave him something to do. He persevered until he had drilled a neat hole two-thirds of the way through the wood.

Next, he took his half-length of wire, broke it into two unequal parts, shaped the shorter piece to form a neat loop with two legs each three or four inches long. He tried to make the loop as near to a perfect circle as possible. The

116

longer piece he wound tightly around the loop so that it formed a close-fitting coil with legs matching the others.

Propping his bench against the wall, he climbed it to the window and examined his handiwork in the glow from outside floodlights, made a few minor adjustments and felt satisfied. He replaced the bench and used the nail to make on its edge two small nicks representing the exact diameter of the loop. Lastly he counted the number of turns to the coil. There were twenty-seven.

It was important to remember these details because in all likelihood he would have to make a second gadget as nearly identical as possible. That very similarity would help to bother the enemy. When a plotter makes two mysterious objects to all intents and purposes the same, it is hard to resist the notion that he knows what he is doing and has a sinister purpose.

To complete his preparations he coaxed the nail back into the place where it belonged. Some time he'd need it again as a valuable tool. They'd never find it and deprive him of it because, to the searcher's mind, anything visibly not disturbed is not suspect.

Carefully he forced the four legs of the coiled loop into the hole that he'd drilled, thus making the square wood function as a supporting base. He now had a gadget, a thingumbob, a means to an end. He was the original inventor and sole proprietor of the Leeming-Finagle something-or-other.

Certain chemical reactions take place only in the presence of a catalyst, like marriages legalised by the presence of an official. Some equations can be solved only by the inclusion of an unknown quantity called X. If you haven't enough to obtain a desired result you've got to add what's needed.

If you require outside help that doesn't exist you must invent it.

Whenever Man had found himself unable to master his environment with his bare hands, thought Leeming, the said environment had been coerced or bullied into submission by Man plus X. That had been so since the beginning of time: Man plus a tool or a weapon.

But X did not have to be anything concrete or solid, it did not have to be lethal or even visible. It could be as intangible and unprovable as the threat of hellfire or the promise of heaven. It could be a dream, an illusion, a whacking great thundering lie—just *anything*.

There was only one positive test: whether it worked.

If it did, it was efficient.

Now to see.

There was no sense in using the Terran language except perhaps as an incantation when one was necessary. Nobody here understood Terran, to them it was just an alien gabble. Besides, his delaying tactic of pretending to be slow to learn the local tongue was no longer effective. They knew that he could speak it almost as well as they could themselves.

Holding the loop assembly in his left hand, he went to the door, applied his ear to the closed spyhole, listened for the sound of patrolling feet. It was twenty minutes before heavy boots came clumping toward him.

"Are you there?" he called, not too loudly but enough to be heard. "Are you there?"

Backing off fast, he lay on his belly on the floor and stood the loop six inches in front of his face.

"Are you there?"

The spyhole clicked open, the light came on, a sour eye looked through.

Completely ignoring the watcher and behaving with the air of one far too absorbed in his task to notice that he was being observed, Leeming spoke through the coiled loop.

"Are you there?"

"What are you doing?" demanded the guard.

Recognising the other's voice, Leeming decided that for once luck must be turning his way. This character, a chump named Marsin, knew enough to point a gun and fire it, or, if unable to do so, yell for help. In all other matters he was not of the elite. In fact Marsin would have to think twice to pass muster as a half-wit.

"What are you doing?" insisted Marsin, raising his voice.

"Calling," said Leeming, apparently just waking up to the other's existence.

"Calling? Calling what or where?"

"Mind your own quilpole business," Leeming ordered, giving a nice display of impatience. Concentrating attention upon the loop, he turned it round a couple of degrees. "Are you there?"

"It is forbidden," insisted Marsin.

Letting go the loud sigh of one compelled to bear fools gladly, Leeming said, "What is forbidden?"

"To call."

"Don't display your ignorance. My species is *always* allowed to call. Where would we be if we couldn't, *enk*?"

That got Marsin badly tangled. He knew nothing about Earthmen or what peculiar privileges they considered essential to life. Neither could he give a guess as to where they'd be without them.

Moreover, he dared not enter the cell and put a stop to whatever was going on. An armed guard was strictly

119

prohibited from going into a cell by himself and that rule had been rigid ever since a fed-up Rigellian had slugged one, snatched his gun and killed six while trying to make a break.

If he wanted to interfere he'd have to go and see the sergeant of the guard and demand that something be done to stop pink-skinned aliens making noises through loops. The sergeant was an unlovely character with a tendency to shout the most intimate details of personal histories all over the landscape. It was the witching hour between midnight and dawn, a time when the sergeant's liver malfunctioned most audibly. And lastly he, Marsin, had proved himself a misbegotten faplap far too often.

"You will cease calling and go to sleep," ordered Marsin with a touch of desperation, "or in the morning I shall report your insubordination to the officer of the day."

"Go ride a camel," Leeming invited. He rotated the loop in manner of one making careful adjustment. "Are you there?"

"I have warned you," Marsin persisted, his only visible eye popping at the loop.

"Fibble off!" roared Leeming.

Marsin shut the spyhole and fibbled off.

As was inevitable after being up most of the night, Leeming overslept. His awakening was abrupt and rude.

The door burst open with a loud crash, three guards plunged in followed by an officer.

Without ceremony the prisoner was jerked off the bench, stripped and shoved into the corridor stark naked. The guards then searched through the clothing while the officer minced around watching them. He was, decided Leeming, definitely a fairy.

Finding nothing in the clothes, they started examining the cell. Right off one of them discovered the loop-assembly and gave it to the officer, who held it gingerly as if it were a bouquet suspected of being a bomb.

Another guard trod on the second piece of wood, kicked it aside and ignored it. They tapped the floor and walls, seeking hollow sounds. Dragging the bench away from the wall, they looked over the other side of it but failed to turn it upside-down and see anything underneath. However, they handled the bench so much that it got on Leeming's nerves and he decided that now was the time to take a walk. He started along the corridor, a picture of nonchalant nudity.

The officer let go a howl of rage and pointed. The guard erupted from the cell, bawled orders to halt. A fourth guard, attracted by the noise, came round the bend of the corridor, aimed his gun threateningly. Leeming turned round and ambled back.

He stopped as he reached the officer, who was now outside the cell and fuming with temper. Striking a modest pose, he said, "Look—*September Morn*."

It meant nothing to the other, who flourished the loop, did a little dance of rage and yelled, "What is this thing?"

"My property," declared Leeming with naked dignity.

"You are not entitled to possess it. As a prisoner of war you are not allowed to have anything."

"Who says so?"

"*I* say so!" informed the fairy somewhat violently.

"Who're you?" asked Leeming, showing no more than academic interest.

"By the Great Blue Sun, I'll show you who I am! Guards, take him inside and——"

"You're not the boss," interrupted Leeming, impressively cocksure. "The Commandant is the boss here. I say so and he says so. If you want to dispute it, let's go ask him."

The guards hesitated, assumed expressions of chronic uncertainty. They were unanimous in passing the buck to the officer. That worthy was taken aback. Staring incredulously at the prisoner, he became wary.

"Are you asserting that the Commandant has given permission for you to have this object?"

"I'm telling you that he hasn't refused permission. Also that it is not for you to give it or refuse it. You roll in your own hog-pen and don't try usurp the position of your betters."

"Hog-pen? What is that?"

"You wouldn't know."

"I shall consult the Commandant about this." Deflated and unsure of himself, the officer turned to the guards. "Put him back in his cell and give him his breakfast as usual."

"How about returning my property, *enk*?" Leeming prompted.

"Not until I have seen the Commandant."

They hustled him into the cell. He got dressed. Breakfast came, the inevitable bowl of slop. He cussed the guards for not making it bacon and eggs. That was deliberate and of malice aforethought. A display of self-assurance and some aggressiveness was necessary to push the game along.

For some reason the tutor did not appear, so he spent the morning furbishing his fluency with the aid of the books. At mid-day they let him into the yard and he could detect no evidence of a special watch being kept upon him while he mingled with the crowd.

The Rigellian whispered, "I got the opportunity to take

another coil of wire. So I grabbed it in case you wanted more." He slipped it across, saw it vanish into a pocket. "That's all I intend to steal. Don't ask me again. One can tempt fate too often."

"What's the matter? Is it getting risky? Are they suspicious of you?"

"Everything is all right so far." He glanced cautiously around. "If some of the other prisoners learn that I'm pinching wire they'll start taking it too. They'll snatch it in the hope of discovering what I intend to do with it, so that they can use it for the same purpose. Two years in prison is two years of education in unmitigated selfishness. Everybody is always on the watch for some advantage, real or imaginary, that he can grab off somebody else. This lousy life brings out the worst in us as well as the best."

"I see."

"A couple of small coils will never be missed," the other went on. "But once the rush starts the stuff will evaporate in wholesale quantities. And that's when all hell will break loose. I daren't take the chance of creating a general ruckus."

"Meaning you fellows can't afford to risk a detailed search right now?" suggested Leeming pointedly.

The Rigellian shied like a frightened horse. "I didn't say that."

"I can put two and two together as expertly as anyone else." Leeming favoured him with a reassuring wink. "I can also keep my mouth shut."

He watched the other mooch away. Then he sought around the yard for more pieces of wood but failed to find any. Oh, well, no matter. At a pinch he could do without. Come to that, he'd darned well have to do without.

The afternoon was given over to linguistic studies on

which he was able to concentrate without interruption. That was one advantage of being in the clink, perhaps the only one. A fellow could educate himself. When the light became too poor and the first pale stars showed through the barred opening in the wall he kicked the door until the sound of it thundered all over the block.

Chapter 8

Feet came running and the spyhole opened. It was Marsin again.

"So it's you, faplap," greeted Leeming. He let go a snort of contempt. "You had to blab, of course. You had to curry favour by reporting me to the officer." He drew himself up to full height. "Well, I am sorry for you. I'd fifty times rather be me than you."

"Sorry for me?" Marsin registered confusion. "Why?"

"Because you are going to suffer."

"*I* am?"

"Yes, you! Not immediately, if that is any consolation. First of all it is necessary for you to undergo the normal period of horrid anticipation. But eventually you are going to suffer. I don't expect you to believe me. All you need do is wait and see."

"It was my duty," explained Marsin semi-apologetically.

"That fact will be considered in mitigation," Leeming

125

assured, "and your agonies will be modified in due proportion."

"I don't understand," complained Marsin, developing a
node of worry somewhere within the solid bone.

"You will—some dire day. So also will those stinking
faplaps who beat me up in the yard. You can inform them
from me that their quota of pain is being arranged."

"I am not supposed to talk to you," said Marsin, dimly
perceiving that the longer he stood by the spyhole the bigger
the fix he got into. "I shall have to go."

"All right. But I want something."

"What is it?"

"I want my bopamagilvie—that thing the officer took
away."

"You cannot have it unless the Commandant gives permission. He is absent today and will not return before tomorrow morning."

"That's no use. I want it now."

"You cannot have it now."

"Forget it." Leeming gave an airy wave of his hand. "I'll
create another one."

"It is forbidden," reminded Marsin very feebly.

"Ha-ha!" said Leeming.

After darkness had grown complete he got the wire from
under the bench and manufactured a second whatzit to all
intents identical with the first one. Twice he was interrupted
but not caught.

That job finished, he up-ended the bench and climbed
it. Taking the newly received coil of wire from his pocket,
he tied one end tightly around the middle bar and hung the
coil outside the window-gap. With spit and dust he cam-
ouflaged the bright tin surface of the one visible strand,
made sure that it could not be seen at farther than nose-tip

distance. He slid down, replaced the bench. The window-gap was so high in the wall that all of its ledge and the bottom three inches of its bars were invisible from below.

Going to the door, he listened and at the right time called, "Are you there?"

When the light came on and the spyhole had opened he got the instinctive feeling that a bunch of them were clustered outside the door, also that the eye in the hole was not Marsin's.

Ignoring everything else, he rotated the loop slowly and carefully, meanwhile calling, "Are you there? Are you there?"

After traversing about forty degrees he paused, gave his voice a tone of intense satisfaction and exclaimed, "So you are there at last! Why don't you keep within easy reach so that we can talk without me having to summon you through a loop?"

Going silent, he put on the expression of one who listens intently. The eye in the spyhole widened, got shoved away, was replaced by another.

"Well," said Leeming, settling himself down for a cosy gossip, "I'll point them out to you first chance I get and leave you to deal with them as you think fit. Let's switch to our own language. There are too many big ears around for my liking." Taking a deep breath, he rattled off at tremendous speed and without pause, "Out sprang the web and opened wide the mirror cracked from side to side the curse has come upon me cried the Lady of——"

Out sprang the door and opened wide and two guards almost fell headlong into the cell in their eagerness to make a quick snatch. Two more posed outside with the fairy glowering between them. Marsin mooned fearfully in the background.

A guard grabbed the loop-assembly, yelled, "I've got it!"

and rushed out. His companion followed at full gallop. Both seemed hysterical with excitement. There was a pause of ten seconds before the door shut. Leeming exploited the fact. Pointing the two middle fingers of one hand at the group, he made horizontal stabbing motions toward them. Giving 'em the Devil's Horns they'd called it when he was a kid. The classic gesture of donating the evil eye.

"There you are," he declaimed dramatically, talking to something that nobody else could see. "Those are the scaly-skinned bums I've been telling you about. They want trouble. They like it, they love it, they dote on it. Give them all they can take."

The whole bunch managed to look alarmed before the door cut them from sight with a vicious slam. Listening at the spyhole, he heard them tramp away muttering steadily between themselves.

Within ten minutes he had broken a length off the coil hanging from the window-bars, restored the spit and dust disguise of the holding strand. Half an hour later he had another neatly made bopamagilvie. Practice was making him expert in the swift and accurate manufacture of these things.

Lacking wood for a base, he used the loose nail to dig a hole in the dirt between the big stone slabs composing the floor of his cell. He rammed the legs of the loop into the hole, twisted the contraption this way and that to make ceremonial rotation easy. Then he booted the door something cruel.

When the right moment arrived he lay on his belly and commenced reciting through the loop the third paragraph of Rule 27, Section 9, Subsection B, of Space Regulations. He chose it because it was a gem of bureaucratic phraseology, a single sentence one thousand words long meaning something known only to God.

"Where refuelling must be carried out as an emergency measure at a station not officially listed as a home-station or definable for special purposes as a home-station under Section A(5) amendment A(5)B the said station shall be treated as if it were definable as a home-station under Section A(5) amendment A(5)B providing that the emergency falls within the authorised list of technical necessities as given in Section J(29-33) with addenda subsequent thereto as applicable to home-stations where such are——"

The spyhole flipped open and shut. Somebody scooted away at top speed. A minute afterward the corridor shook to what sounded like a massed cavalry charge. The spyhole again opened and shut. The door crashed inward.

This time they reduced him to his bare pelt, searched his clothes, raked the cell from end to end. Their manner was that of those singularly lacking in brotherly love. Turning the bench upside-down, they tapped it, knocked it, kicked it, did everything but run a large magnifying glass over it.

Watching this operation, Leeming encouraged them by emitting a sinister snigger. There had been a time when he could not have produced a sinister snigger even to win a very large bet. But he could do it now. The ways in which a man can rise to the occasion are without limit.

Giving him a look of sudden death and total destruction, a guard went out, staggered back with a heavy ladder, mounted it and suspiciously surveyed the window-gap. As an intelligent examination it was a dead loss because his mind was concerned only with the solidity of the bars. He grasped each bar with both hands and shook vigorously. His fingers did not touch the thread of wire nor did his eyes detect it. Satisfied, he got down and tottered out with the ladder.

The others departed. Leeming dressed himself, listened at the spyhole. Just a very faint hiss of breath and occasional rustle of clothes nearby. He sat on the bench and waited. In short time the lights blazed on and the spyhole popped open.

Stabbing two fingers toward the hole, he declaimed, "Die, faplap!"

The hole snapped shut. Feet moved away, stamping much too loudly. He waited. After half an hour of complete silence the eye offered itself again and for its pains received another two-fingered curse. Five minutes later it had yet another bestowed upon it. If it was the same eye all the time it was a glutton for punishment.

This game continued at erratic intervals for four hours before the eye had had enough. Leeming immediately made another coiled-loop, gabbled through it at the top of his voice and precipitated another raid. They did not strip him and search the cell this time. They contented themselves with confiscating the gadget. And they showed symptoms of aggravation.

There was just enough wire left for one more blood-pressure booster. He decided to keep it against a future need and get some sleep. Inadequate food and not enough slumber were combining to make inroads upon his physical reserves.

Flopping full length on the bench, he sighed and closed red-rimmed eyes. In due time he started snoring fit to saw through the bars. That caused a panic in the passage and brought the gang along in another rush.

Wakened by the uproar, he damned them to perdition. Then he lay down again. He was plain bone-tuckered—but so were they.

* * *

He slept solidly until mid-day without a break except for the usual lousy breakfast. Then came the usual lousy dinner. At exercise time they kept him locked in. He hammered and kicked on the door, demanded to know why he wasn't being allowed to walk in the yard, shouted threats of glandular dissection for all and sundry. They took no notice.

So he sat on the bench and thought things over. Perhaps this denial of his only measure of freedom was a form of retaliation for making them hop around like agitated fleas in the middle of the night. Or perhaps the Rigellian was under suspicion and they'd decided to prevent contact.

Anyway, he had got the enemy bothered. He was messing them about single-handed, far behind the lines. That was something. The fact that a combatant is a prisoner doesn't mean he's out of the battle. Even behind thick walls he can still harass the foe, absorbing his time and energy, undermining his morale, pinning down at least a few of his forces.

The next step, he concluded, was to widen and strengthen the curse. He must do it as comprehensively as possible. The more he spread it and the more ambiguous the terms in which he expressed it, the more plausibly he could grab the credit for any and every misfortune that was certain to occur sooner or later.

It was the technique of the gypsy's warning. People tend to attach specific meanings to ambiguities when circumstances arise and shape themselves to give especial meanings. People don't have to be very credulous, either. It is sufficient for them to be made expectant, with a tendency to wonder—after the event.

"In the near future a tall, dark man will cross your path."

After which any male above average height, and not a

blond, fits the picture. And any time from five minutes to five years is accepted as the near future.

"Mamma, when the insurance man called he really smiled at me. *Do you remember what the gypsy said?*"

To accomplish anything worth while one must adapt to one's own environment. If the said environment is radically different from everyone else's the method of accommodating to it must be equally different. So far as he knew he, Leeming, was the only Terran in this prison and the only prisoner held in solitary confinement. Therefore his tactics could have nothing in common with any schemes the Rigellians had in mind.

The Rigellians were up to something, no doubt of that. They wouldn't be wary and secretive about nothing. It was almost a dead-sure bet that they were digging a tunnel. Probably a bunch of them were deep in the earth right now, scraping and scratching without tools. Removing dirt and rock a few pounds at a time. Progress at the rate of a pathetic two or three inches per night. A constant, never-ending risk of discovery, entrapment and perhaps some insane shooting. A year-long project that could be terminated in minutes with a shout and a chatter of automatic guns.

But to get out of a strong stone cell in a strong stone jail one doesn't have to make a desperate and spectacular escape. If sufficiently patient, resourceful, glib and cunning, one can talk the foe into opening the doors and pushing one out.

Yes, you can use the wits that God has given you.

By law of probability various things must happen within and without the prison, not all of them pleasing to the enemy. Some officer must get the galloping gripes right under his body-belt. Or a guard must fall down a watchtower ladder and break a leg. Somebody must lose a wad of money or his pants or his senses. Farther afield a bridge must collapse, or a train get derailed, or a spaceship crash at take-off. Or there'd be an explosion in a munitions factory. Or a military leader would drop dead.

He'd be playing a trump card if he could establish his claim as the author of most of this trouble. The essential thing was to stake it in such a way that they could not effectively combat it, neither could they exact retribution in a torture-chamber.

The ideal strategy was to convince the enemy of his malevolence in a way that would equally convince them of their own impotence. If he succeeded—and it was a big *if*—they would come to the logical conclusion that the only method of getting rid of constant trouble would be to get rid of Leeming, alive and in one piece. If—and it was a big *if*—he could link cause and effect irrevocably together they'd have to remove the cause in order to dispose of the effect.

The question of how exactly to achieve this fantastic result was a jumbo problem that would have appalled him back home. In fact he'd have declared it impossible despite that the basic lesson of space-conquest is that nothing is impossible. But by now he'd had three lonely months in which to incubate a solution—and the brain becomes wonderfully stimulated by grim necessity. It was a good thing that he had an idea in mind; he had a mere ten minutes before the time came to apply it.

The door opened, a trio of guards scowled at him and one of them rasped, "The Commandant wishes to see you at once. Amash, faplap!"

Leeming walked out saying, "Once and for all, I am not a faplap, see?"

The guard booted him in the buttocks.

* * *

The Commandant lolled behind a desk with a lower rank-ing officer seated on either side. He was a heavily built specimen. His lidless, horn-covered eyes gave him a frigid, unemotional appearance as he studied the prisoner.

Leeming calmly sat himself on a handy chair and the officer on the right immediately bellowed, "Stand to atten-tion in the presence of the Commandant!"

Making a gesture of contradiction, the Commandant said boredly, "Let him sit."

A concession at the start, thought Leeming. Curiously he eyed a wad of papers on the desk. Probably a complete report of his misdeeds, he guessed. Time would show. Any-way, he had one or two weapons with which to counter theirs. It would be a pity, for instance, if he couldn't exploit their ignorance. The Allies knew nothing about the Zan-gastans. By the same token the Zangastans knew little or nothing about several Allied species, Terrans included. In coping with him they were coping with an unknown quan-tity.

And from now on it was a quantity doubled by the addi-tion of X.

"I am given to understand that you now speak our lan-guage," began the Commandant.

"Not much use denying it," Leeming confessed.

"Very well. You will give us information concerning yourself."

"I have given it already. I gave it to Major Klavith."

"That is no concern of mine. You will answer my ques-tions and your answers had better be truthful." Positioning an official form upon his desk, he held his pen in readiness. "Name of planet of origin?"

"Earth."

The other wrote it phonetically in his own script, then continued, "Name of race?"

"Terran."

"Name of species?"

"*Homo nosipaca*," said Leeming, keeping his face straight.

Writing it down, the Commandant looked doubtful, asked, "What does that mean?"

"Space-traversing Man," Leeming informed.

"H'm!" The other was impressed despite himself. "Your personal name?"

"John Leeming."

"John Leeming," repeated the Commandant, putting it down.

"And Eustace Phenackertiban," added Leeming airily.

That was written down also, though the Commandant had some difficulty in finding suitable hooks and curlicues to express Phenackertiban. Twice he asked Leeming to repeat the alien cognomen and that worthy obliged.

Studying the result, which resembled a Chinese recipe for rotten egg gumbo, the Commandant said, "Is it your custom to have two sets of names?"

"Most certainly," Leeming assured. "We can't avoid it seeing that there are two of us."

Twitching the eyebrows he didn't possess, the listener showed mild surprise. "You mean that you are always conceived and born in pairs? Two identical males or females every time?"

"No, no, not at all." Leeming adopted the air of one about to state the obvious. "Whenever one of us is born he immediately acquires a Eustace."

"A Eustace?"

"Yes."

The Commandant frowned, picked his teeth, glanced at the other officers. If he was seeking inspiration he was out of luck; they put on the blank expressions of fellows who'd come along merely to keep company.

"What," asked the Commandant at long last, "is a Eustace?"

Gaping at him in open incredulity, Leeming said, "You don't know?"

"I am putting the questions. You will provide the answers. What is a Eustace?"

Leeming informed, "An invisibility that is part of one's self."

Understanding dawned on the Commandant's scaly face. "Ah, you mean a soul? You give your soul a separate name?"

"Nothing of the sort. I have a soul of my own and Eustace has a soul of his own." He added as an afterthought, "At least, I hope we have."

The Commandant lay back in his chair and stared at him. There was quite a long silence during which the side officers continued to play dummies.

Finally the Commandant admitted, "I do not understand."

"In that case," announced Leeming, irritatingly triumphant, "it is evident that you have no alien equivalent of Eustaces yourselves. You're all on your own. Just single-lifers. That's your hard luck."

Slamming a hand on the desk, the Commandant gave his voice a bit more military whoof and demanded, "Exactly what is a Eustace? Explain to me as clearly as possible!"

"I'm in poor position to refuse the information," Leeming conceded with hypocritical reluctance. "Not that it matters much. Even if you gain perfect understanding there is nothing you can do about it."

"That remains to be seen," opined the Commandant,

looking bellicose. "Cease evading the issue and tell me all that you know about these Eustaces."

"Every Earthling lives a double life from birth to death," said Leeming. "He exists in close mental association with an entity that always calls himself Eustace something-or-other. Mine happens to be Eustace Phenackertiban."

"You can actually *see* this entity?"

"No, never at any time. I cannot see him, smell him or feel him."

"Then how do you know that this is not a racial delusion?"

"Firstly, because every Terran can hear his own Eustace. I can hold long conversations with mine, providing that he happens to be within reach, and I can hear him speaking clearly and logically within the depths of my mind."

"You cannot hear him with the ears?"

"No, only with the mind. The communication is telepathic, or to be more accurate, quasi-telepathic."

"I can believe that," informed the Commandant with considerable sarcasm. "You have been heard talking out loud, shouting at the top of your voice. Some telepathy, *enk*?"

"When I have to boost my thoughts to get range I can do it better by expressing them in words. People do the same when they sort out a problem by talking to themselves. Haven't you ever talked to yourself?"

"That is no business of yours. What other proof have you that a Eustace is not imaginary?"

Taking a deep breath, Leeming went determinedly on. "He has the power to do many things after which there is visible evidence that those things have been done." He shifted attention to the absorbed officer sitting on the left. "For example, if my Eustace had a grudge against this officer and advised me of his intention to make him fall downstairs, and if before long the officer fell downstairs and broke his neck——"

"It could be mere coincidence," the Commandant scoffed.

"It could," agreed Leeming. "But there can be far too many coincidences. If a Eustace promises that he is going to do forty or fifty things in succession and all of them happen he is either doing them as promised or he is a most astounding prophet. Eustaces don't claim to be prophets. Nobody visible or invisible can foresee the future with such detailed accuracy."

"That is true enough."

"Do you accept the fact that you have a father and mother?"

"Of course," admitted the Commandant.

"You don't consider it strange or abnormal?"

"Certainly not. It is inconceivable that one should be born without parents."

"Similarly we accept the fact that we have Eustaces and we cannot conceive the possibility of existing without them."

The Commandant thought it over, said to the right-hand officer, "This smacks of mutual parasitism. It would be interesting to learn what benefit they derive from each other."

"It's no use asking what my Eustace gets out of me," Leeming chipped in. "I can't tell you because I don't know."

"You expect me to believe that?" asked the Commandant, behaving like nobody's fool. He showed his teeth. "On your own evidence you can talk with him. Why have you never asked him?"

"We Terrans got tired of asking that question long, long ago. The subject has been dropped and the situation accepted."

"Why?"

"The answer is always the same. Eustaces readily admit

that we are essential to their existence but cannot explain how because they've no way of making us understand."

"That could be an excuse, a self-preservative evasion," the Commandant offered. "They won't tell you because they don't want you to know."

"Well, what do you suggest we do about it?"

Dodging that one, the Commandant went on, "What benefit do *you* get out of the association? What good is your Eustace to *you*?"

"He provides company, comfort, information, advice and——"

"And what?"

Bending forward, hands on knees, Leeming practically spat it at him. "If necessary, vengeance!"

That struck home good and hard. The Commandant rocked back, displaying a mixture of ire and scepticism. The two under-officers registered disciplined apprehension. It's a hell of a war when one can be chopped down by a ghost.

Pulling himself together, the Commandant forced a grim smile as he pointed out, "You're a prisoner. You've been under detention a good many days. Your Eustace doesn't seem to have done much about it."

"Not yet," agreed Leeming happily.

"What d'you mean, not yet?"

"As one free to roam at will on an enemy world he had enough top-priority jobs to keep him busy for a piece. He's been doing plenty and he'll do plenty more, in his own time and his own way."

"Is that so? And what does he intend to do?"

"Wait and see," Leeming advised with formidable confidence.

That did not fill them with delight.

"Nobody can imprison more than half a Terran," he went

on. "The solid, visible, tangible half. The other half cannot be pinned down by any method whatsoever. It is beyond anyone's control. It wanders loose collecting information of military value, indulging a little sabotage, doing just as it pleases. You've created that situation and you're stuck with it."

"We created it? We didn't invite you to come here. You dumped yourself on us unasked."

"I had no choice about it because I had to make an emergency landing. This could have been a friendly world. It isn't. Who's to blame for that? If you insist on fighting with the Combine against the Allies you must accept the consequences—including whatever a Eustace sees fit to do."

"Not if we kill you," said the Commandant nastily.

Leeming gave a disdainful laugh. "That would make matters fifty times worse."

"In what way?"

"The life-span of a Eustace is longer than that of his Terran partner. When a man dies his Eustace takes seven to ten years to disappear from existence. We have an ancient song to the effect that old Eustaces never die, they only fade away. Our world holds thousands of lonely, disconnected Eustaces gradually fading."

"So——?"

"Kill me and you'll isolate my Eustace here with no man or other Eustace for company. His days will be numbered and he'll know it. He'll have nothing to lose, being no longer restricted by consideration of my safety. Because I've gone for keeps he'll be able to eliminate me from his plans and give his undivided attention to anything he chooses." He eyed the listeners as he finished, "It's a safe bet that he'll run amok and create an orgy of destruction. Remember, you're an alien lifeform to him. He'll have no feelings or compunctions with regard to you."

The Commandant reflected in silence. It was exceedingly difficult to believe all this, and his prime instinct was to reject it lock, stock and barrel. But before space-conquest it had been equally difficult to believe things more fantastic but now accepted as commonplace. He dare not dismiss it as nonsense; the time had long gone by when anyone could afford to be dogmatic. The space adventurings of all the Combine and the Allied species had scarcely scratched one galaxy of an unimaginable number composing the universe; none could say what incredible secrets were yet to be revealed, including, perhaps, such etheric entities as Eustaces.

Yes, the stupid believe things because they are credulous—or they are credulous because stupid. The intelligent do not blindly accept but, being aware of their own ignorance, neither do they reject. Right now the Commandant was acutely aware of general ignorance concerning this lifeform known as Terrans. It *could* be that they were dual creations, half-Joe, half-Eustace.

"All this is not impossible," he decided ponderously, "but it appears to me somewhat improbable. There are more than twenty lifeforms associated with us in the Combine. I do not know of one that exists in natural copartnership with another."

"The Lathians do," contradicted Leeming, mentioning the leaders of the opposition, the chief cause of the war.

The Commandant was suitably startled. "You mean they have Eustaces too?"

"No, I don't. They have something similar but inferior. Each Lathian is unconsciously controlled by an entity that calls itself Willy something-or-other. They don't know it, of course. We wouldn't know it if our Eustaces hadn't told us."

"How did they find out?"

"As you know, the biggest battles to date have all been fought in the Lathian sector. Both sides have taken prisoners. Our Eustaces told us that each Lathian prisoner had a controlling Willy but was blissfully unaware of it." He grinned, added, "They made it plain that a Eustace doesn't think much of a Willy. Apparently a Willy is a pretty low form of associated life."

Frowning, the Commandant said, "This is something definite, something we should be able to check for ourselves. But how are we going to do it if the Lathians are ignorant of this state of affairs?"

"Easy as pie," Leeming offered. "They are holding a bunch of Terran prisoners. Get someone to ask those prisoners, separately and individually, whether the Lathians have the Willies."

"We'll do just that," snapped the Commandant, his manner that of one about to call a bluff. He turned to the right-hand officer. "Bajashim, beam a signal to our chief liaison officer at Lathian H.Q. and order him to question those prisoners."

"You can double-check while you're at it," interjected Leeming, "just to clinch it. To us, anyone who shares his life with an invisible being is known as a Nut. Ask the prisoners whether all the Lathians are Nuts."

"Take note of that and have it asked as well," ordered the Commandant. He returned attention to Leeming. "Since you could not anticipate your forced landing and capture, and since you have been kept in close confinement, there is no possibility of collusion between you and the Terran prisoners far away."

"That's right."

"Therefore I shall weigh your evidence in the light of what replies come to my signal." He stared hard at the other. "If those replies fail to confirm your statements I'll know that you are a shameless liar in some respects and probably a liar in all respects. Here, we have special and very effective methods of dealing with liars."

"That's to be expected. But if the replies do confirm me you'll know that I've told the truth, won't you?"

"No," said the Commandant savagely.

It was Leeming's turn to be shocked. "Why not?"

Thinning his lips, the Commandant growled, "As I have remarked, there cannot possibly have been any direct communication between you and other Terran prisoners. However, that means nothing. There can have been collusion between your Eustace and their Eustaces."

Bending sidewise, he jerked open a drawer, placed a loop-assembly on the desk. Then another and another. A bunch of them.

"Well," he invited with malicious triumph, "what have you to say to that?"

Chapter 9

Leeming went into something not far off a momentary panic. He could see what the other meant. He could talk to his Eustace, who in turn could talk to other Eustaces. And the other Eustaces could talk to their imprisoned partners.

Get yourself out of that!

He had an agile mind but after three months of semi-starvation it was tending to lose pace. Lack of adequate nourishment was telling on him already; his thoughts plodded at the very time he wanted them to sprint.

The three behind the desk were waiting for him, watching his face, counting the seconds he needed to produce an answer. The longer he took to find one the weaker it would be. The quicker he came up with something good the more plausible it would sound. Cynical satisfaction was creeping into their faces and he was inwardly frantic by the time he saw an opening and grabbed at it.

"You're wrong on two counts."

"State them."

"Firstly, one Eustace cannot communicate with another over a distance so enormous. His mental output just won't reach that far. To talk from world to world he has to have the help of a Terran who, in his turn, has radio equipment available."

"We've only your word for that," the Commandant reminded. "If a Eustace *can* communicate without limit it would be your best policy to conceal the fact. You would be a fool to admit it."

"I cannot do more than give you my word regardless of whether or not you credit it."

"I do not credit it—yet."

"No Terran task force has rushed to my rescue, as would happen had my Eustace told them about me."

"Pfah!" said the Commandant. "It would take them much longer to get here than the time you have spent as a prisoner. Probably twice as long. And then only if by some miracle they managed to avoid being shot to pieces on the way. The absence of a rescue party means nothing." He waited for a response that did not come, finished, "If you have anything else to say it had better be convincing."

"It is," assured Leeming. "And we don't have my word for it. We have yours."

"Nonsense! I made no statements concerning Eustaces."

"On the contrary, you have said that there could be collusion between them."

"What of it?"

"There can be collusion only if Eustaces really exist, in which case my evidence is true. But if my evidence is false, then Eustaces do not exist and there cannot possibly be a conspiracy between non-existent things."

The Commandant sat perfectly still while his face took

on a faint shade of purple. He looked and felt like a trapper trapped. The left-hand officer wore an expression of one struggling hard to suppress a disrespectful snicker.

"If," continued Leeming, piling it on for good measure, "you do not believe in Eustaces then you cannot logically believe in conspiracy between them. On the other hand, if you believe in the possibility of collusion then you've got to believe in Eustaces. That is, of course, if you're in bright green breeches and your right mind."

"Guard!" roared the Commandant. He pointed an angry finger. "Take him back to his cell." Obediently they started hustling the prisoner through the door when he changed his mind and bawled, "Halt!" Snatching up a loop-assembly, he waved it at Leeming. "Where did you get the material with which to make this?"

"My Eustace brought it for me. Who else?"

"Get out of my sight!"

"Merse, faplap!" urged the guards, prodding with their guns. "Amash! Amash!"

The rest of that day and all the next one he spent sitting or lying on the bench, reviewing what had taken place, planning his next moves and in lighter moments admiring his own ability as a whacking great liar.

Now and again he wondered how his efforts to battle his way to freedom with his tongue compared with Rigellian attempts to do it with bare hands. Who was making the most progress? Of great importance, who, once out, would stay out? One thing was certain: his method was less tiring to the underfed and weakened body, though more exhausting to the nerves.

Another advantage was that for the time being he had side-tracked their intention of squeezing him for military information. Or had he? Possibly from their viewpoint his revelations concerning the dual nature of Terrans were infinitely more important than details of armaments, which data might be false anyway. All the same, he had avoided for a time what might otherwise have been a rough and painful interrogation. By thus postponing the agony he had added brilliance to the original gem of wisdom, namely, that baloney baffles brains.

Just for the ducks of it he bided his time and, when the spyhole opened, let it catch him in the middle of giving grateful thanks to Eustace for some weird service not specified. As intended, this got the jumpy Marsin to wondering who had arrived at the crossroads and copped some of Eustace's dirty work. Doubtless the sergeant of the guard would speculate about the same matter before long. And in due course so would the officers.

Near midnight, with sleep still evading him, it occurred to him that there was no point in doing things by halves. If a thing is worth doing it is worth doing well—and that applies to lying or to any form of villainy as much as to anything else. Why rest content merely to register a knowing smile whenever the enemy suffered a petty misfortune?

His tactics could be extended much farther than that. No form of life was secure from the vagaries of chance. Good fortune came along as well as bad, in any part of the cosmos. There was no reason why Eustace should not snatch the credit for both. No reason why he, Leeming, should not take unto himself the implied power to reward as well as to punish.

That wasn't the limit, either. Good luck and bad luck are positive phases of existence. He could cross the neutral zone and confiscate the negative phases. Through Eustace he could assign to himself not only the credit for things done, good or bad, but also for things *not* done. In the pauses between staking claims to things that happened he could exploit those that did not happen.

The itch to make a start right now was irresistible. Rolling off the bench, he belted the door from top to bottom. The guard had just been changed, for the eye that peered in was that of Kolum, a character who had bestowed a kick in the rump not so long ago. Kolum was a cut above Marsin, being able to count upon all twelve fingers if given sufficient time to cogitate.

"So it is you!" said Leeming, showing vast relief. "I am very glad of that. I befriended you in the hope that he would lay off you, that he would leave you alone for at least a little while. He is far too impetuous and much too drastic. I can see that you are more intelligent than the other guards and therefore able to change for the better. Indeed, I have pointed out to him that you are obviously too civilised to be a sergeant. He is difficult to convince but I am doing my best for you."

"Huh?" said Kolum, half flattered, half scared.

"So he's left you alone at least for the time being," Leeming said, knowing that the other was in no position to deny it. "He's done nothing to you—yet." He increased the gratification. "I'll do my very best to keep control of him. Only the stupidly brutal deserve slow death."

"That is true," agreed Kolum eagerly. "But what——"

"Now," interrupted Leeming with firmness, "it is up to you to prove that my confidence is justified and thus protect yourself against the fate that is going to visit the slower-witted. Brains were made to be used, weren't they?"

"Yes, but——"

"Those who don't possess brains cannot use what they haven't got, can they?"

"No, they cannot, but——"

"All that is necessary to demonstrate your intelligence is to take a message to the Commandant."

Kolum popped his eyes in horror. "It is impossible. I dare not disturb him at this hour. The sergeant of the guard will not permit it. He will——"

"You are not being asked to take the message to the Commandant immediately. It is to be given to him personally when he awakens in the morning."

"That is different," said Kolum, vastly relieved. "But I must warn you that if he disapproves of the message he will punish you and not me."

"He will not punish me lest I in turn punish him," assured Leeming, as though stating a demonstrable fact. "Write my message down."

Leaning his gun against the corridor's farther wall, Kolum dug pencil and paper out of a pocket. A strained expression came into his eyes as he prepared himself for the formidable task of inscribing a number of words.

"To The Most Exalted Lousy Screw," began Leeming.

"What does 'lousy screw' mean?" asked Kolum as he struggled to put down the strange Terran words phonetically.

"It's a title. It means 'Your Highness'. Man, how high he is!" Leeming pinched his nose while the other pored over the paper. He continued to dictate, going very slowly to keep pace with Kolum's literary talent. "The food is insufficient and very poor in quality. I am physically weak, I have lost much weight and my ribs are beginning to show. My Eustace does not like it. The thinner I get the more threatening he becomes. The time is fast approaching when I shall have to refuse all responsibility for his actions. Therefore I beg Your Most Exalted Lousy Screwship to give serious consideration to this matter."

"There are many words and some of them long ones," complained Kolum, managing to look like a reptilian martyr. "I shall have to rewrite them more readably when I go off duty."

"I know and I appreciate the trouble you are taking on my behalf." Leeming bestowed a beam of fraternal fondness. "That's why I feel sure you'll live long enough to do the job."

"I must live longer than that," insisted Kolum, popping the eyes again. "I have the right to live, haven't I?"

"That is precisely the argument I've been using," said Leeming in the manner of one who has striven all night to establish the irrefutable but cannot yet guarantee success.

"I cannot talk to you any longer," informed Kolum, picking up his gun. "I am not supposed to talk to you at all. If the sergeant of the guard should catch me he will——"

"The sergeant's days are numbered," Leeming told him in judicial tones. "He will not live long enough to know he's dead."

His hand extended in readiness to close the spyhole, Kolum paused, looked as if he'd been slugged with a sockful of wet sand. Then he said, "How can *anyone* live long enough to know that he's dead?"

"It depends on the method of killing," assured Leeming. "There are some you've never heard of and cannot imagine."

At this point Kolum found the conversation distasteful. He closed the spyhole. Leeming returned to the bench, sprawled upon it. The light went out. Seven stars peeped through the window-slot—and they were not unattainable.

In the morning breakfast came an hour late but consisted of one full bowl of lukewarm pap, two thick slices of brown bread heavily smeared with grease and a large cup of warm liquid vaguely resembling paralysed coffee. He got through the lot with mounting triumph. By contrast with what they had been giving him this feast made the day seem like Christmas. His spirits perked up with the fullness of his belly.

No summons to a second interview came that day or the next. The Commandant made no move for more than a week. Evidently His Lousy Screwship was still awaiting a reply from the Lathian sector and did not feel inclined to take further action before he received it. However, meals remained more substantial, a fact that Leeming viewed as positive evidence that someone was insuring himself against disaster.

Then early one morning the Rigellians acted up. From the cell they could be heard but not seen. Every day at about an hour after dawn the tramp of their two thousand pairs of feet sounded somewhere out of sight and died away toward the workshops. Usually that was all that could be heard, no voices, no desultory conversation, just the weary trudge of feet and an occasional bellow from a guard.

This time they came out singing, their raucous voices holding a distinct touch of defiance. They were bawling in thunderous discord something about Asta Zangasta's a dirty old geezer, got fleas on his chest and sores on his beezer. It should have sounded childish and futile. It didn't. The corporate effort seemed to convey an unspoken threat.

Guards yelled at them. Singing rose higher, the defiance increasing along with the volume. Standing below his window-slot, Leeming listened intently. This was the first mention he'd heard of the much-abused Asta Zangasta, presumably this world's king, emperor or leading hooligan.

The bawling of two thousand voices rose crescendo. Guards screamed frenziedly and were drowned within the din. Somewhere a warning shot was fired. In the watch-towers the guards edged their guns around, dipped them as they aimed into the yard.

"Oh, what a basta is Asta Zangasta!" hollered the distant Rigellians as they reached the end of their epic poem.

There followed blows, shots, scuffling sounds, howls of fury. A bunch of twenty fully armed guards raced flat-footed past Leeming's window, headed for the unseeable fracas. The uproar continued for half an hour before gradually it died away. Resulting silence could almost be felt.

At exercise-time Leeming had the yard to himself, there being not another prisoner in sight. He mooched around, puzzled and gloomy, until he encountered Marsin on yard-patrol.

"Where are the others? What has happened to them?"

"They misbehaved and wasted a lot of time. They are being detained in the workshops until they have made up the loss in production. It is their own fault. They started work late for the deliberate purpose of slowing down output. We didn't even have time to count them."

Leeming grinned into his face. "And some guards were hurt?"

"Yes," Marsin admitted.

"Not severely," Leeming suggested. "Just enough to give them a taste of what is to come. Think it over!"

"What do you mean?"

"I meant what I said—think it over." Then he added, "But *you* were not injured. Think that over too!"

He ambled away, leaving Marsin uneasy and bewildered. Six times he trudged around the yard while doing some heavy thinking himself. Sudden indiscipline among the Rigellians certainly had stirred up the prison and created enough excitement to last a week. He wondered what had caused it. Probably they'd done it to gain relief from incarceration and despair. Sheer boredom can drive people into performing the craziest tricks.

On the seventh time round he was still pondering when suddenly a remark struck him with force like the blow of a hammer. *"We had not time even to count them."* Holy smoke! *That* must be the motive of this morning's rowdy performance. The choral society had avoided a count. There could be only one reason why they should wish to dodge the regular numbering parade.

Finding Marsin again, he promised, "Tomorrow some of you guards will wish you'd never been born."

"Are you threatening us?"

"No, I am making a prophetic promise. Tell the guard officer what I have said. Tell the Commandant, too. It might help you to escape the consequences."

"I will tell them," said Marsin, mystified but grateful.

The following morning proved that he had been one hundred per cent correct in his supposition that the Rigellians were too shrewd to invite thick ears and black eyes without good reason. It had taken the enemy a full day to arrive at the same conclusion.

At one hour after dawn the Rigellians were marched out dormitory by dormitory, in batches of fifty instead of the usual continuous stream. They were counted in fifties, the easy way. This simple arithmetic became thrown out of kilter when one dormitory produced only twelve prisoners, all of them sick, weak, wounded or otherwise handicapped.

Infuriated guards rushed indoors to drag out the absent thirty-eight. They weren't there. The door was firm and solid, the window-bars intact. Guards did considerable confused galloping around before one of them detected the slight shift of a well-trampled floor-slab. They lugged it up, found underneath a narrow but deep shaft from the bottom of which ran a tunnel. With great unwillingness one of them went down the shaft, crawled into the tunnel and in due time emerged a good distance outside the walls. Needless to say he had found the tunnel empty.

Sirens wailed, guards pounded all over the jail, officers shouted contradictory orders, the entire place began to resemble a madhouse. The Rigellians got it good and hard for spoiling the previous morning's count and thus giving the escapees a full day's lead. Boots and gun-butts were freely used, bodies dragged aside badly battered and unconscious.

The surviving top-ranker of the offending dormitory, a lieutenant with a severe limp, was held responsible for the break, charged, tried, sentenced, put against a wall and shot. Leeming could see nothing of this but did hear the hoarse commands of "Present . . . aim . . . fire!" and the following volley.

He prowled round and round his cell, clenching and unclenching his fists, his stomach writhing like a sack of snakes and swearing mightily to himself. All that he wanted, all that he prayed for was a high-ranking Zangastan throat under his thumbs. The spyhole flipped open but hastily shut before he could spit into somebody's eye.

The upset continued without abate as inflamed guards searched all dormitories one by one, testing doors, bars, walls, floors and even the ceilings. Officers screamed bloodthirsty threats at sullen groups of Rigellians who were slow to respond to orders.

At twilight outside forces dragged in seven tired, bedraggled escapees who'd been caught on the run. Their reception was short and sharp. "Present . . . aim . . . fire!" Frenziedly

Leeming battered at his door but the spyhole remained shut and nobody answered. Two hours later he made another coiled loop with the last of his wire. He spent half the night talking into it menacingly and at the top of his voice. Nobody took the slightest notice.

By noon next day a feeling of deep frustration had come over him. He estimated that the Rigellian break-out must have taken most of a year to prepare. Result: eight dead and thirty-one still loose. If they kept together and did not scatter the thirty-one could form a crew large enough to seize a ship of any size up to and including a space-destroyer. But on the basis of his own experiences he thought they had remote chance of making such a theft.

With the whole world alarmed by an escape of this size there'd be a strong military screen at every spaceport and it would be maintained until the last of the thirty-one had been rounded up. The free might stay free for quite a time if they were lucky, but they were planet-bound, doomed to ultimate recapture and subsequent execution.

Meanwhile their fellows were getting it rough in consequence and his own efforts had been messed up. He did not resent the break, not one little bit. Good luck to them. But if only it had taken place two months earlier or later.

Moodily he finished his dinner, when four guards came for him. "The Commandant wants you at once." Their manner was edgy and subdued. One wore a narrow bandage around his scaly pate, another had a badly swollen eye.

Just about the worst moment to choose, thought Leeming. The Commandant would be all set to go up like a rocket at first hint of opposition of any kind. You cannot argue with a brasshat in a purple rage; emotion comes uppermost, words are disregarded, logic is treated with contempt. He was going to have a tough job on his hands.

The four marched him along the corridor, two in front, two behind. Left, right, left, right, thud, thud, thud—it made him think of a ceremonial parade to the guillotine. Around the corner in a little triangular yard there should be waiting a priest, a hanging knife, a wicker basket, a wooden box.

Together they tramped into the same room as before. The Commandant was sitting behind his desk but there were no junior officers in attendance. The only other person present was an elderly civilian occupying a chair on the Commandant's right; he studied the prisoner with a sharp, intent gaze as he entered and took a seat.

"This is Pallam," introduced the Commandant with amiability so unexpected that it dumbfounded the listener. Showing a touch of awe, he added, "He has been sent here by no less a person that Zangasta himself."

"A mental specialist, I presume?" invited Leeming, wary of a trap.

"Nothing like that," said Pallam quietly. "I am especially interested in all aspects of symbiosis."

Leeming's back hairs stirred. He did not like the idea of being cross-examined by an expert. Such characters had penetrating, unmilitary minds and a pernicious habit of destroying a good story by exhibiting its own contradictions. This mild-looking civilian, he decided, was definitely a major menace.

"Pallam wishes to ask you a few questions," informed the Commandant, "but those will come later." He put on a self-satisfied expression. "For a start I wish to say that I am indebted for the information you gave at our previous interview."

"You mean that it has proved useful to you?" asked Leeming, hardly believing his ears.

"Very much so in view of this serious and most stupid mutiny. All the guards responsible for Dormitory Fourteen are to be drafted to battle areas where they will be stationed upon spaceports liable to attack. That is their punishment for gross neglect of duty." He gazed thoughtfully at the other, went on, "My own fate would have been no less had not Zangasta considered the escape a minor matter when compared with the important data I got from you."

Though taken by surprise, Leeming was swift to cash in. "But when I asked, you saw to it personally that I had better food. Surely you expected some reward?"

"Reward?" The Commandant was taken aback. "I did not think of such a thing."

"So much the better," approved Leeming, admiring the other's magnanimity. "A good deed is trebly good when done with no ulterior motive. Eustace will take careful note of that."

"You mean," put in Pallam, "that his code of ethics is identical with your own?"

Damn the fellow! Why did he have to put his spoke in? Be careful now!

"Similar in some respects but not identical."

"What is the most outstanding difference?"

"Well," said Leeming, playing for time, "it's hard to decide." He rubbed his brow while his mind whizzed dizzily. "I'd say in the matter of vengeance."

"Define the difference," ordered Pallam, sniffing along the trail like a hungry bloodhound.

"From my viewpoint," informed Leeming, inwardly cursing the other to hell and perdition, "he is unnecessarily sadistic."

There, that gave needed coverage for any widespread claims it might be desirable to make later on.

"In what way?" persisted Pallam.

"My instinct is to take prompt action, to get things over and done with. His tendency is to prolong the agony."

"Explain further," pressed Pallam, making a thorough nuisance of himself.

"If you and I were mortal enemies, if I had a gun and you had not, I would shoot and kill you. But if Eustace had you marked for death he'd make it slower, more gradual."

"Describe his method."

"First, he'd let you know that you were doomed. Then he'd do nothing about it until eventually you became obsessed with the notion that it was all an illusion and that nothing ever would be done. At that point he'd remind you with a minor blow. When resulting fear and alarm had worn off he'd strike a harder one. And so on and so on with increasing intensity spread over as long a time as necessary."

"Necessary for what?"

"Until your doom became plain and the strain of waiting for it became too much to bear." He thought a moment, added, "No Eustace ever has killed anyone. He uses tactics peculiarly his own. He arranges accidents or he chivvies a victim into dying by his own hand."

"He drives a victim to suicide?"

"Yes, that's what I've said."

"And there is no way of avoiding such a fate?"

"Yes there is," Leeming contradicted. "At any time the victim can gain personal safety and freedom from fear by redressing the wrong he has done to that Eustace's partner."

"Such redress immediately terminates the vendetta?"

"That's right."

"Whether or not you approve personally?"

"Yes. If my grievance ceases to be real and becomes only

imaginary, my Eustace refuses to recognise it or do anything about it."

"So what it boils down to," said Pallam pointedly, "is that his method provides motive and opportunity for repentance while yours does not?"

"I suppose so."

"Which means that he has a more balanced sense of justice?"

"He can be darned ruthless," objected Leeming, momentarily unable to think of a retort less feeble.

"That is beside the point," snapped Pallam. He lapsed into meditative silence, then remarked to the Commandant, "It seems that the association is not between equals. The invisible component is also the superior one. In effect, it is the master of a material slave but exercises mastery with such cunning that the slave would be the first to deny his own status."

He shot a provocative glance at Leeming, who set his teeth and said nothing. Crafty old hog, thought Leeming—if he was trying to tempt the prisoner into a heated denial he was going to be disappointed. Let him remain under the delusion that Leeming had been weighed in the balance and found wanting. There is no shame in being defined as inferior to a figment of one's own imagination.

Now positively foxy, Pallam probed, "When your Eustace takes it upon himself to wreak vengeance he does so because circumstances prevent suitable punishment being administered either by yourself or the Terran community? Is that correct?"

"Near enough," admitted Leeming cautiously.

"In other words, he functions only when you and the law are impotent?"

"He takes over when the need arises."

"You are being evasive. We must get this matter straight. If you or your fellows can and do punish someone, does any Eustace also punish him?"

"No," said Leeming, fidgeting uneasily.

"If you or your fellows cannot or do not punish someone does a Eustace then step in and enforce punishment?"

"Only if a living Terran has suffered unjustly."

"The sufferer's Eustace takes action on his partner's behalf?"

"Yes."

"Good!" declared Pallam. He leaned forward, watched the other keen-eyed and managed to make his attitude intimidating. "Now let us suppose that your Eustace finds justifiable reason to punish another Terran—*what does the victim's Eustace do about it?*"

Chapter 10

It was a clever trap based upon the knowledge that questions about factual, familiar, everyday things can be answered automatically, almost without thought. Whereas a liar seeking a supporting lie needs time to create consistency. It should have got Leeming completely foozled. That it did not do so was no credit to his own wits.

While his mind still whirled his mouth opened and the words "Not much" popped out of their own accord. For a mad moment he wondered whether Eustace had arrived and joined the party.

"Why not?"

Encouraged by his tongue's mastery of the situation, Leeming gave it free rein. "I have told you before and I am telling you again that no Eustace will concern himself for one moment with a grievance that is wholly imaginary. A Terran who is guilty of a crime has no genuine cause for complaint. He has brought vengeance upon himself and the

161

cure lies in his own hands. If he doesn't enjoy suffering he need only get busy and undo whatever wrong he has done to another."

"Will his Eustace urge or influence him to take action necessary to avoid punishment?"

"Never having been a criminal myself," answered Leeming with great virtue, "I am unable to tell you. I suppose it would be near the truth to say that Terrans behave because association with Eustaces compels them to behave. They have little choice about the matter."

"On the other hand, Terrans have no way of compelling their Eustaces to behave?"

"No compulsion is necessary. A Eustace will always listen to his partner's reason and act within the limits of common justice."

"As I told you," said Pallam in an aside to the Commandant, "the Terran is the lower form of the two." He returned attention to the prisoner. "All that you have told us is acceptable because it is consistent—as far as it goes."

"What d'you mean, as far as it goes?"

"Let me take it to the bitter end," suggested Pallam. "I do not see any rational reason why any criminal's Eustace should allow his partner to be driven to suicide. Since they are mutually independent of others but mutually dependent upon each other, a Eustace's inaction is contrary to the basic law of survival."

"Nobody commits suicide until he has gone off his rocker."

"Until he has done what?"

"Become insane," said Leeming. "An insane person is worthless as a material partner. To a Eustace he is already dead, not worth protecting or avenging. Eustaces associate only with the sane."

Pouncing on that, Pallam said excitedly, "So the benefit

they derive is rooted somewhere within Terran minds? It is mental sustenance that they draw from you?"

"I don't know."

"Does your Eustace ever make you feel tired, exhausted, perhaps a little stupefied?"

"Yes," said Leeming with emphasis. How true, brother, how true. Right now he'd find pleasure in choking Eustace to death.

"I would like to pursue this phenomenon for months," Pallam told the Commandant. "It is an absorbing subject. There are no records of symbiotic association among anything higher than the plants and six species of the lower *elames*. To find it among the higher vertebrates, sentient forms, and one of them intangible, is remarkable, truly remarkable."

The Commandant looked impressed without knowing what the other was talking about.

"Give him your report," urged Pallam.

"Our liaison officer, Colonel Shomuth, has replied from the Lathian sector," the Commandant told Leeming. "He is fluent in Cosmoglotta and therefore was able to question many Terran prisoners without the aid of a Lathian interpreter. We sent him a little more information and the result is significant."

"What else did you expect?" Leeming observed, inwardly consumed with curiosity.

Ignoring that, the Commandant went on, "He reported that most of the prisoners refused to make comment or to admit anything. They maintained determined silence. That is understandable because nothing could shake their belief that they were being tempted to surrender information of military value. They resisted all of Colonel Shomuth's persuasions and kept their mouths shut." He sighed at such stubbornness. "But some talked."

"A few are always willing to blab," remarked Leeming.

"Certain officers talked, including Cruiser Captain Tompass . . . Tompus . . ."

"Thomas?"

"Yes, that is the word." Swivelling around in his chair, the Commandant pressed a wall-button. "This is the beamed interview unscrambled and recorded on tape."

A crackling hiss poured out of a perforated grid set in the wall. It grew louder, died down to a background wash. Voices came out of the grid.

Shomuth: "Captain Thomas, I have been ordered to check certain information now in our possession. You have nothing to lose by giving answers, nothing to gain by refusing them. There are no Lathians present, only the two of us. You may speak freely and what you say will be treated in confidence."

Thomas: "Mighty leery about the Lathians all of a sudden, aren't you? You won't fool me with that gambit. Enemies are enemies no matter what their name or shape. Go trundle your hoop—you'll get nothing out of me."

Shomuth, patiently: "I suggest, Captain Thomas, that you hear and consider the questions before you decide whether or not to answer them."

Thomas, boredly: "All right. What d'you want to know?"

Shomuth: "Whether our Lathian allies really are Nuts."

Thomas, after a long pause: "You want the blunt truth?"

Shomuth: "We do."

Thomas, with a trace of sarcasm: "I hate to speak against anyone behind his back, even a lousy Lathian. But there are times when one is compelled to admit that dirt is dirt, sin is sin, and a Lathian is what he is, eh?"

Shomuth: "Please answer my question."

Thomas: "The Lathians are nuts."

Shomuth: "And they have the Willies?"

Thomas: "Say, where did you dig up this information?"

Shomuth: "That is our business. Will you be good enough to give me an answer?"

Thomas, belligerently: "Not only have they got the willies but they'll have a darned sight more of them before we're through."

Shomuth, puzzled: "How can that be? We have learned that each and every Lathian is unconsciously controlled by a Willy. Therefore the total number of Willies must be limited. It cannot be increased except by the birth of more Lathians."

Thomas, quickly: "You've got me wrong. What I meant was that as Lathian casualities mount up the number of unattached Willies will increase. Obviously even the best of Willies cannot control a corpse, can he? There will be lots more Willies loafing around in proportion to the number of Lathian survivors."

Shomuth: "Yes, I see what you mean. And it will create a psychic problem of great seriousness." Pause. "Now, Captain Thomas, have you any reason to suppose that a large number of partnerless Willies might be able to seize control of another and different lifeform? Such as my own species, for example?"

Thomas, with enough menace to deserve a space-medal: "I wouldn't be surprised."

Shomuth: "You don't know for sure?"

Thomas: "No."

Shomuth: "It is true, is it not, that you are aware of the real Lathian nature only because you have been warned of it by your Eustace?"

Thomas, startled: "By my *what*?"

Shomuth: "By your *Eustace*. Why should that surprise you?"

Thomas, recovering swiftly enough to earn a bar to the medal: "I thought you said Useless. Silly of me. Yes, my Eustace. You're dead right there."

Shomuth, in lower tones: "There are more than four hundred Terran prisoners here. That means more than four hundred Eustaces wandering around unchallenged on this planet. Correct?"

Thomas: "I am unable to deny it."

Shomuth: "The Lathian heavy cruiser *Veder* crashed on landing and was a total loss. The Lathians attributed it to an error of judgment on the part of the crew. But that was just three days after you prisoners were brought here. Was it a mere coincidence?"

Thomas, scintillating: "Work it out for yourself."

Shomuth: "You realise that so far as we are concerned your refusal to reply is as good as an answer?"

Thomas: "Construe it any way you like. I will not betray Terran military secrets."

Shomuth: "All right. Let me try you on something else. The biggest fuel dump in this part of the galaxy is located a few degrees south of here. A week ago it blew up to total destruction. The loss was a severe one; it will handicap the Combine fleets for quite a time to come."

Thomas, with enthusiasm: "Cheers!"

Shomuth: "Lathian technicians theorise that a static spark caused a leaking tank to explode and that set off the rest in rapid succession. We can always trust technicians to come up with a glib explanation."

Thomas: "Well, what's wrong with it?"

Shomuth: "That dump has been established for more than

four years. No static sparks have caused trouble during that time."

Thomas: "What are you getting at?"

Shomuth, pointedly: "You have admitted yourself that more than four hundred Eustaces are roaming this area, free to do as they please."

Thomas, in tones of stern patriotism: "I am admitting nothing. I refuse to answer any more questions."

Shomuth: "Has your Eustace prompted you to say that?"

Silence.

Shomuth: "If your Eustace is now present, can I question him through you?"

No reply.

Switching off, the Commandant said, "There you are. Eight other Terran officers gave more or less the same evidence. The rest tried to conceal the facts but, as you have heard, they failed. Zangasta himself has listened to the taped records and is deeply concerned about the situation."

"He needn't worry his head about it," Leeming offered.

"Why not?"

"It's all a lot of bunk, a put-up job. There was collusion between my Eustace and theirs."

The Commandant looked sour. "As you emphasised at our last meeting, there cannot be collusion without Eustaces, so it makes no difference either way."

"I'm glad you can see it at last."

"Let it pass," chipped in Pallam impatiently. "It is of no consequence. The confirmatory evidence is adequate no matter how we look at it."

Thus prompted, the Commandant continued, "I have been doing some investigating myself. In two years we've had a long series of small-scale troubles with the Rigellians, none of them really serious. But after you arrived there comes a big break that obviously must have been planned long before you turned up but soon afterward took place in circumstances suggesting outside help. Whence came this assistance?"

"Not telling," said Leeming knowingly.

"At one time or another eight of my guards earned your enmity by assaulting you. Of these, four are now in hospital badly injured, two more are to be drafted to the fighting front. I presume that it is only a matter of time before the remaining two are plunged into trouble?"

"The other two have arbitrated and earned forgiveness. Nothing will happen to them."

"Is that so?" The Commandant registered surprise.

Leeming went on, "I cannot give the same guarantee with respect to the firing squad, the officer in charge of it or the higher-up who ordered that helpless prisoners be shot."

"We *always* execute prisoners who break out of jail. It is an old-established practice and a necessary deterrent."

"We always settle accounts with the executioners," Leeming gave back. "It is an old-established practice and a necessary deterrent."

"By 'we' you mean you and your Eustace?" put in Pallam.

"Yes."

"Why should your Eustace care? The victims were not Terrans. They were merely a bunch of obstreperous Rigellians."

"Rigellians are allies. And allies are friends. I feel bad about the cold-blooded, needless slaughtering of them. Eustace is very sensitive to my emotions."

"But not necessarily obedient to them?"

"No."

168

"In fact," pressed Pallam, determined to establish the point once and for all, "if there is any question of one being subordinate to the other, it is *you* who serves *him*."

"Most times, anyway," conceded Leeming with the air of having a tooth pulled.

"Well, it confirms what you've already told us." Pallam gave a thin smile. "The chief difference between Terrans and Lathians is that you know you're controlled, whereas the Lathians are ignorant of their own status."

"We are not controlled consciously or unconsciously," Leeming insisted. "We exist in mutual partnership the same as you do with your wife. Sometimes she gives way to you, other times you give way to her. Neither of you bothers to estimate who has given way the most in any specific period and neither of you insists that a perfect balance must be maintained. That's how it is. And it's mastery by neither party."

"I wouldn't know, never having been mated." Pallam turned to the Commandant. "Carry on."

"As probably you are aware by now, this planet has been set aside as the Combine's main penal world," informed the Commandant. "Already we hold a large number of prisoners, mainly Rigellian."

"What of it?"

"There are more to come. Two thousand Centaurians and six hundred Thetans are due to arrive and fill a new jail next week. Combine forces will transfer more enemy lifeforms as soon as we have accommodation ready for them and ships are available." He eyed the other speculatively. "It is only a matter of time before they start dumping Terrans on us as well."

"Is the prospect bothering you?"

"Zangasta has decided that he must refuse to accept Terrans."

"That's up to him," said Leeming, blandly indifferent.

"Zangasta has a clever mind," opined the Commandant, oozing patriotic admiration. "He is of the firm opinion that to assemble a formidable army of mixed prisoners all on one planet, and then add some thousands of Terrans to the mixture, is to create a potentially dangerous situation. He foresees trouble on a scale vaster than we could handle. Indeed, we might lose control of this world, strategically placed in the Combine's rear, and become subject to the violent attacks of our own allies."

"That is quite possible," Leeming agreed. "In fact it's quite probable. In fact it's practically certain. But it's not Zangasta's only worry. It's the one he's seen fit to put out for publication. He's got a private one too."

"And what is that?"

"Zangasta himself originated the order that escaped prisoners be shot. He must have done so—otherwise nobody would dare shoot them. Now he's jumpy because a Eustace may be sitting on his bed and grinning at him every night. He thinks that a few thousand Eustaces will be a proportionately greater menace to him. But he's wrong."

"Why is he wrong?" inquired the Commandant.

"Because it isn't only the repentant who have no cause to fear. The dead haven't either. The arrival on this world of fifty million Eustaces means nothing whatever to a corpse. Zangasta had better countermand that shooting order if he wants to go on living."

"I'll inform him of your remarks. However, such cancellation may not be necessary. As I have told you, he is clever. He has devised a subtle strategy that will put all your evidence to the final, conclusive test and at the same time may solve his problems to his own satisfaction."

Feeling vague alarm, Leeming asked, "Am I permitted to know what he intends to do?"

"He has given instructions that you be told. And already he has swung into action." The Commandant waited for the sake of effect, then finished, "He has beamed the Allies a proposal to exchange prisoners."

Leeming fidgeted around in his seat. Ye gods, the plot was thickening with a vengeance. From the very beginning his sole purpose had been to talk himself out of jail and into some other situation more favourable for sudden departure at high speed. He'd been trying to lift himself over the wall with his tongue. Now they were taking his story and plastering it all over the galaxy. Oh, what a tangled web we weave when first we practise to deceive!

"What is more," the Commandant went on, "the Allies have notified us of their acceptance providing we exchange rank for rank. That is to say, captains for captains, navigators for navigators and so forth."

"That's reasonable."

"Zangasta," said the Commandant, grinning like a hungry wolf, "has agreed in his turn—providing that the Allies take Terran prisoners first and make exchange on a basis of two for one. He is now awaiting their reply."

"Two for one?" echoed Leeming, blinking. "You mean he wants them to release two of their prisoners for every Terran they get back?"

"No, no, of course not." He increased the grin and exposed the roots of his teeth. "They must return two Combine troopers for each Terran and his Eustace that we had back. That is two for two and perfectly fair, is it not?"

"It's not for me to say." Leeming swallowed hard. "The Allies are the judges."

"Until a reply arrives and mutual agreement has been achieved, Zangasta wishes you to have better treatment. You will be transferred to the officers' quarters outside the walls, you will share their meals and be allowed to go walks in the country. Temporarily you will be treated as a non-combatant and you'll be very comfortable. It is necessary that you give me your parole not to try to escape."

Holy smoke, this was another stinker. The entire fiction was shaped toward ultimate escape. He couldn't abandon it now. Neither was he willing to give his word of honour with the cynical intention of breaking it.

"Parole refused," he said firmly.

The Commandant was incredulous. "Surely you do not mean that?"

"I do. I have no choice. Terran military law does not permit a prisoner-of-war to give such a promise."

"Why not?"

"Because no Terran can accept responsibility for his Eustace. How can I swear not to get out when half of me cannot be got in? Can a twin take oath on behalf of his brother?"

"Guard!" called the Commandant, visibly disappointed.

He mooched uneasily around his cell for a full twelve days, occasionally chatting with Eustace night-times for the benefit of ears lurking outside the door. Definitely he'd wangled himself into a predicament that was a case of put up or shut up; in order to put up he dared not shut up.

The food remained better in quantity though little could be said for its quality. Guards treated him with that diffidence accorded to captives who somehow are in cahoots with their superiors. Four more recaptured Rigellians were brought back but not shot. All the signs and portents were that he'd still got a grip on the foe.

Though he'd said nothing to them, the other prisoners had got wind of the fact that in some mysterious way he was responsible for the general softening of prison conditions. At exercise-time they treated him as a deep and subtle character who could achieve the impossible. From time to time their curiosity got the better of them.

"You know they didn't execute those last four?"

"Yes," Leeming admitted.

"It's being said that you stopped the shooting."

"Who says so?"

"It's just a story going around."

"That's right, it's just a story going around."

"I wonder why they shot the first bunch but not the second. There must be a reason."

"Maybe the Zangastans have developed qualms of conscience even if belatedly," Leeming suggested.

"There's more to it than that."

"Such as what?"

"Somebody has shaken them up."

"Who, for instance?"

"I don't know. There's a strong rumour that you've got the Commandant eating out of your hand."

"That's likely, isn't it?" Leeming countered.

"I wouldn't think so. But one never knows where one is with the Terrans." The other brooded a bit, asked, "What did you do with that wire I stole for you?"

"I'm knitting it into a pair of socks. Nothing fits better or wears longer than solid wire socks."

Thus he foiled their noseyness and kept silence, not wanting to arouse false hopes. Inwardly he was badly bothered. The Allies in general and Earth in particular knew nothing whatever about Eustaces and therefore were likely to treat a two-for-one proposition with the contempt it deserved. A blank refusal on their part might cause him to be plied with awkward questions impossible to answer.

In that case it would occur to them sooner or later that they were afflicted with the biggest liar in history. They'd then devise tests of fiendish ingenuity. When he flunked them the balloon would go up.

He wasn't inclined to give himself overmuch credit for kidding them along so far. The few books he'd been able to read had shown that Zangastan religion was based upon reverence for ancestral spirits. The Zangastans were also familiar with what is known as poltergeist phenomena. The ground had been prepared for him in advance; he'd merely ploughed it and sown the crop. When a victim already believes in two kinds of invisible beings it isn't hard to persuade him to swallow a third.

But when the Allies beamed Asta Zangasta a curt invitation to make his bed on a railroad track it was possible that the third type of spirit would be regurgitated with violence. Unless by fast, convincing talk he could cram it back down their gullets when it was halfway out. How to do that?

In his cell he was stewing this problem over and over when the guards came for him again. The Commandant was there but Pallam was not. Instead, a dozen civilians eyed him curiously. That made a total of thirteen enemies, a very suitable number to pronounce him ready for the chopper.

Feeling as much the centre of attention as a six-tailed wombat at the zoo, he sat down and four civilians immediately started chivvying him, taking it in relays. They were interested in one subject and one only, namely, bopamagilvies. It seemed that they'd been playing for hours with his samples, had achieved nothing except some practice in acting daft, and were not happy about it.

On what principle did a bopamagilvie work? Did it focus telepathic output into a narrow, long-range beam? At what distance did his Eustace get beyond range of straight conversation and have to be summoned with the aid of a gadget? Why was it necessary to make directional search before obtaining a reply? How did he know how to make a coiled-loop in the first place?

"I can't explain. How does a bird know how to make a nest? The knowledge is wholly instinctive. I have known how to call my Eustace ever since I was old enough to shape a piece of wire."

"Could it be that your Eustace implants the necessary knowledge in your mind?"

"Frankly, I've never given that idea a thought. But it is possible."

"Will any kind of wire serve?"

"So long as it is non-ferrous."

"Are all Terran loops of exactly the same construction and dimensions?"

"No, they vary with the individual."

"We've made careful and thorough search of Terran prisoners held by the Lathians. Not one of them owns a similar piece of apparatus. How do you account for that?"

"They don't need one."

"Why not?"

"Because when more than four hundred of them are imprisoned together they can always count on at least a few of their Eustaces being within easy reach at any given time."

Somehow he beat them off, feeling hot in the forehead and cold in the belly. Then the Commandant took over.

"The Allies have flatly refused to accept Terran prisoners

ahead of other species, or to exchange them two for one, or to discuss the matter any further. What have you to say to that?"

Steeling himself, Leeming commented, "Look, on your side there are more than twenty lifeforms, of which the Lathians and the Zebs are by far the most powerful. Now if the Allies had wanted to give priority of exchange to one species do you think the Combine would agree? If, for example, the favoured species happened to be the Tansites, would the Lathians and Zebs vote for them to get home first?"

A tall, authoritative civilian chipped in. "I am Daverd, personal aide to Zangasta. He is of your own opinion. He believes that the Terrans have been outvoted. Therefore I am commanded to ask you one question."

"What is it?"

"Do your allies know about your Eustaces?"

"No."

"You have succeeded in hiding the facts from them?"

"There's never been any question of concealing anything from them. With friends the facts just don't become apparent. Eustaces take effective action only against enemies and that is something that cannot be concealed for ever."

"Very well." Daverd came closer, put on a conspiratorial air. "The Lathians started this war and the Zebs went with them by reason of their military alliance. The rest of us got dragged in for one reason or another. The Lathians are strong and arrogant but, as we now know, they are not responsible for their actions."

"What's this to me?"

"Separately we numerically weaker lifeforms cannot stand against the Lathians or the Zebs. But together we are strong enough to step out of the war and maintain our right to be neutral. So Zangasta has consulted the others."

Lord! Isn't it amazing what can be done with a few yards of copper wire?

"He has received their replies today," Daverd went on. "They are willing to make a common front for the sake of enjoying mutual peace—providing that the Allies are equally willing to recognise their neutrality and exchange prisoners with them."

"Such sudden unanimity among the small fry tells me something pretty good," observed Leeming with malice.

"It tells you what?"

"Allied forces have won a major battle lately. Somebody has been given a hell of a lambasting."

Daverd refused to confirm or deny it. "You are the only Terran we hold on this planet. Zangasta thinks he can make good use of you."

"How?"

"He has decided to send you back to Terra. It will be your task to persuade them to agree to our plans. If you fail, a couple of hundred thousand hostages will suffer— remember that!"

"The prisoners have no say in this matter, no hand in it, no responsibility for it. If you vent your spite upon them a time will surely come when you'll be made to pay—remember *that*!"

"The Allies will know nothing about it," Daverd retorted. "There will be no Terrans and no Eustaces here to inform them by any underhanded method. Henceforth we are keeping Terrans out. The Allies cannot use knowledge they do not possess."

"No," agreed Leeming. "It's quite impossible to employ something you haven't got."

* * *

They provided a light destroyer crewed by ten Zangastans. With one stop for refuelling and the fitting of new tubes it took him to a servicing planet right on the fringe of the battle area. This dump was a Lathian outpost, but those worthies showed no interest in what their smaller allies were up to, neither did they realise that the one Terranlike creature really was a Terran. They got to work relining the destroyer's tubes in readiness for its journey home. Meanwhile, Leeming was transferred to an unarmed one-man Lathian scout-ship. The ten Zangastans officiously saluted before they left him.

From this point he was strictly on his own. Take-off was a heller. The seat was far too big and shaped to fit the Lathian backside, which meant that it was humped in the wrong places. The controls were unfamiliar and situated too far apart. The little ship was fast and powerful but responded differently from his own. How he got up he never knew, but he made it.

After that there was the constant risk of being tracked by Allied detector stations and blown apart in full flight. He charged among the stars hoping for the best and left his beam transmitter severely alone; calls on an enemy frequency might make him a dead duck in no time at all.

He arrowed straight for Terra. His sleeps were restless and uneasy. The tubes were not to be trusted despite that flight-duration would be only a third of that done in his own vessel. The strange autopilot was not to be trusted merely because it was of alien design. The ship itself was not to be trusted for the same reason. The forces of his own side were not to be trusted because they'd tend to shoot first and ask questions afterward.

More by good luck than good management he penetrated

the Allied front without interception. It was a feat that the foe could accomplish, given the audacity, but had never attempted because the risk of getting into Allied territory was as nothing to the trouble of getting out again.

In due time he came in fast on Terra's night side and plonked the ship down in a field a couple of miles west of the main spaceport. It would have been foolish to take a chance by landing a Lathian vessel bang in the middle of the port. Somebody behind a heavy gun might have stuttered with excitement and let fly.

The moon was shining bright along the Wabash when he approached the front gate afoot and a sentry bawled, "Halt! Who goes there?"

"Lieutenant Leeming and Eustace Phenackertiban."

"Advance and be recognised."

He ambled forward thinking to himself that such an order was manifestly dunderheaded. Be recognised. The sentry had never seen him in his life and wouldn't know him from Myrtle McTurtle. Oh, well, baloney baffles brains.

At the gate a powerful cone of light shone down upon him. Somebody with three chevrons on his sleeve emerged from a nearby hut bearing a scanner on the end of a thin, black cable. He waved the scanner over the arrival from head to foot, concentrating mostly upon the face.

A loudspeaker in the hut ordered, "Bring him into Intelligence H.Q."

They started walking.

The sentry let go an agitated yelp. "Hey, where's the other guy?"

"What guy?" asked the sergeant, stopping and staring around.

"Smell his breath," Leeming advised.

"You gave me *two* names," asserted the sentry, full of resentment.

"Well, if you ask the sergeant nicely he'll give you two more," said Leeming. "Won't you, Sarge?"

"Let's get going," growled the sergeant, displaying liverish impatience.

They reached Intelligence H.Q. The duty officer was Colonel Farmer. He gaped at Leeming and said, "Well!" He said it seven times.

Without preamble, Leeming demanded, "What's all this about us refusing to make a two-for-one swap for Terran prisoners?"

Farmer appeared to haul himself with an effort out of a fantastic dream. "You know of it?"

"How could I ask if I didn't?"

"All right. Why should we accept such a cockeyed proposition? We're in our right minds, you know!"

Bending over the other's desk, hands splayed upon it, Leeming said, "All we need do is agree—upon one condition."

"What condition?"

"That they make a similar agreement with respect to Lathians. Two of our men for one Lathian and one Willy."

"One *what*?"

"One Willy. The Lathians will take it like birds. They have been propaganding all over the shop that one Lathian is worth two of anything else. They're too conceited to refuse such an offer. They'll advertise it as proof positive that even their enemies know how good they are."

"But——" began Farmer, slightly dazed.

"Their allies will fall over themselves in their haste to agree also. They'll do it from different motives to which the Lathians will wake up when it's too late. Try it for size. Two of our fellows for one Lathian and his Willy."

Farmer stood up, his belly protruding, and roared, "What the blue blazes is a Willy?"

"You can easily find out," assured Leeming. "Consult your Eustace."

Showing alarm, Farmer lowered his tones to a soothing pitch and said as gently as possible, "Your appearance here has been a great shock to me. Many months ago you were reported missing and believed killed."

"I crash-landed and got taken prisoner in the back of beyond. They were a snake-skinned bunch called Zangastans. They slung me into the jug."

"Yes, yes," said Colonel Farmer, making pacifying gestures. "But how on earth did you get away?"

"Farmer, I cannot tell a lie—I hexed them with my bopamagilvie."

"Huh?"

"So I left by rail," informed Leeming, "and there were ten faplaps carrying it." Taking the other unaware, he let go a vicious kick at the desk and made a spurt of ink leap across the blotter. "Now let's see some of the intelligence they're supposed to have in Intelligence. Beam the offer. Two for a cootie-coated Lathian and a Willie Terwilliger." He stared around, a wild look in his eyes. "And find me someplace to sleep—I'm dead beat."

Holding himself in enormous restraint, Farmer said, "Lieutenant, is that the proper way in which to talk to a colonel?"

"One talks in *any* way to anybody. Mayor Snorkum will lay the cake. Go paddle a poodle." Leeming kicked the desk again. "Get busy and tuck me into bed."